NO LONGER A DREAM

Ever since Harry, Cat had steered clear of emotional attachments. But she didn't know what to make of the well-known film magnate, Caleb Steele. Why did everything between them become so personal? And why wouldn't he just leave her alone, to get on with her job?

NO LONGER A DREAM

BY
CAROLE MORTIMER

MILLS & BOON LIMITED
15–16 BROOK'S MEWS
LONDON W1A 1DR

First published in Great Britain 1986
by Mills & Boon Limited

© Carole Mortimer 1986

Australian copyright 1986
Philippine copyright 1986
This edition 1986

ISBN 0 263 75307 7

Set in Monophoto Plantin 11 on 11½ pt.
01-0386 – 45570

Made and printed in Great Britain by
Richard Clay (The Chaucer Press) Ltd,
Bungay, Suffolk

For John
Matthew and Joshua

CHAPTER ONE

'YOU have a delicious body, one of the most perfect I've ever seen, but I'm not in the mood for you right now, so could you get out of bed and get some clothes on?'

The velvet roughness of that American-accented voice, and the things it was saying, were enough to wake Cat from her heavy sleep, but it was the sharp slap on the tender flesh of her bottom that caused her lids to fly open.

For a moment she just lay there, the feel of the chocolate-brown silk sheet beneath her, sensuous against her nakedness. Nakedness! She looked down sharply, sure she blushed from head to toe as she saw she was indeed completely naked. She looked away quickly, falling on to her back, only to see herself again in the smoky brown glass of the mirrors directly above her. The whole ceiling was covered in mirrors!

Where was she? And who had that silky rough voice belonged to?

She was alone in the room now, so she could only put the questions to herself. And a couple of dozen more like them! Who's bedroom was this? What was she doing here? Who had undressed her? And *why?*

The last seemed the easiest to answer. Her first time in bed with a man and she didn't even remember it, didn't even remember the *man!* She covered her eyes with a groan, feeling sick.

'It must have been some party.' The velvety voice spoke with harsh amusement. 'Would you like me to get you a hair-of-the-dog?'

She lowered her arm, didn't actually need to turn in the man's direction, could see his reflection in the mirrored ceiling. He was as naked as she was!

'Have you gone back to sleep?' he prompted hardly.

She wished she could sink through a hole in the floor and disappear, at the very least go back to sleep and forget this had ever happened. But she doubted she would ever sleep peacefully again, would always be frightened this nightmare was going to be repeated. For it had to be a dream; she didn't wake up in the bedrooms of men she didn't even recognise, let alone remember!

'I can see that you haven't.' He moved to stand over her, looking down at her. 'I realise that you probably have a terrible hangover, but you've only yourself to blame.'

His voice definitely lacked sympathy, and Cat blinked hard as she looked up at him, unaware of just how much like her name she looked at that moment, her tumble of long blonde curls wilder than usual after a night in bed, her green eyes still sleepy.

'Do you know where the bedclothes are?' Her voice was a pained rasp, her throat feeling totally devoid of moisture, her tongue swollen and dry.

Dark brows rose over cold black eyes. 'On the

floor where you kicked them last night.' He was totally indifferent to the fact that neither of them was wearing a stitch of clothing. 'You're a restless sleeper.'

She wasn't usually—but then she had never shared a bed with anyone for the night before! She took advantage of his turned back, as he looked through the wardrobe that took up the whole of one wall, to pull the sheet from the floor over her body and up to her chin, sitting up to watch the man over its softness.

He had thick black hair, lightly sprinkled with grey, a finer, softer looking hair covering the whole of his body, and it was the rest of that body that made Cat gulp. This man was lean and powerful rather than muscular, his shoulders wide, his back taut with strength, his waist slender, his buttocks a muscular curve to his body, his legs long and fleshless. He was completely at ease, and yet the latent power was there.

Had she experienced that power? She didn't *feel* any different, but then that was no guarantee; maybe you weren't supposed to feel different! She had spent the last twenty-four years 'saving herself' and now she didn't even know what she had saved herself for!

The man turned impatiently. 'Are you going to stay in there all day?'

The fact that she had never seen a man's body this intimately before was nothing to the shock she received when her embarrassed gaze finally reached his face. Caleb Steele! She couldn't believe it, but she would know that harshly

attractive face anywhere. Even when he was
standing across the room from her stark naked!

Black hair that was usually meticulously
brushed back from his face fell forward in a damp
swathe, eyebrows the same jet-black jutting out
over cold black eyes, his nose an arrogant slash
between high cheekbones, his sculptured mouth a
hard, forbidding line. At almost forty he looked
older, a cynical twist to his mouth, the same
emotion reflected in those chilling eyes. He was
also considered one of the most powerful—and
dangerous—men in Hollywood!

He shrugged at her lack of reply, turning back
to the wardrobe, taking a brown silk shirt from a
hanger to shrug his shoulders into it. 'Breakfast is
out in the dining room. If you want any I would
advise you to get up and get dressed,' he rasped.
'I don't sit down to eat with women who are only
half-dressed!'

Caleb Steele, owner of the Steele film studios,
an exclusive hotel and casino in Lake Tahoe, and
with tremendous influence in some quarters of
the media. He was also the man she had come to
the party last night to meet. Well she had met
him; God, how she had met him!

She cleared her throat painfully. 'Mr Steele——'

He turned around, tucking the dark brown
shirt into the waist of black trousers, before
sliding the zip up with a firm movement,
his hands dropping down to his hips. 'Caleb,'
he bit out in that Atlantic drawl. 'Mr Steele is
a little formal in the circumstances. That is
my bed you're lying in,' he pointed out
mockingly.

She squeezed her eyes shut, but he was still there when she opened them again. She had guessed it had to be this man's room, from the sinfully mirrored ceiling, to the wide double bed, and erotic silk sheets. He gave the impression of a man who liked to be comfortable when he took his pleasure with a woman.

'You also seem to have me at a disadvantage.' He quirked those rugged dark brown brows enquiringly.

Oh my God, he didn't even know her name! 'I'm Cat,' she told him flatly. 'Catherine Howard. And I've heard all the Henry the Eighth jokes I need, thank you.' This occasion neither warranted nor necessitated one of the endless jokes she had been subjected to concerning her name over the years.

The firmly moulded lips didn't move by a fraction of an inch, and yet something, she thought it was the expression in his eyes, told Cat that he was amused. She agreed, this was hardly the time for outright laughter, about anything!

'Was she one of the ones that lost her head?' he derided, dealing with his unruly hair now as he stood in front of the mirror gracing the big oak dressing-table, looking more like the photographs Cat had seen of him: the film mogul that made even the most temperamental director or actor quake in their shoes.

She had attended the party given by this man's son with such high hopes after Luke Steele told her his father was going to 'show up' some time during the evening, knowing that Caleb Steele was probably the only man who could get her an

interview with his father, Lucien Steele, the
writer. Maybe if she had satisfied him in bed he
still could, she thought bitterly.

'Yes,' she snapped, knowing that history
claimed Henry the Eighth's fifth wife had even
been guilty of the adultery he had accused her of,
unlike a couple of the others, who had just
outlived their attraction. 'Was I—satisfactory?'
she asked with much more bravado than she felt.
They said that your subconscious would only let
you do what you really wanted to do; had she
wanted to go to bed with this man that caused a
shiver of apprehension down her spine even
though he had only been casually mocking?

He slowly replaced the brush on the dressing-
table before turning to look at her, arching one
dark brow, the black eyes unfathomable. 'Don't
you know?' he asked softly, that black gaze
looking at her with new interest, playing over the
tumble of honey-blonde hair, deep green eyes
shadowed with embarrassment now, the small
classical nose, and wide kissable mouth, only her
shoulders bared to his view now as she clutched
the sheet tightly to her, although the warmth of
his gaze as it moved to meet hers seemed to say
he approved of what he could see.

Cat moistened her mouth nervously. 'I—er—I
think someone must have put something in one
of my drinks.' Her throat was getting easier
now, although she knew the reason for its
dryness only too well. 'I only drink orange
juice, you see.' She became flushed at his
sceptical snort. 'It's true,' she insisted indignantly. 'I'm allergic to alcohol!'

'What happens when you drink it?' His eyes were narrowed now.

She grimaced. 'I pass out.'

He gave a derisive inclination of his head. 'That would seem to be what you did.'

Before or after? She swallowed down her growing feelings of panic. 'I tell you my drinks must have been tampered with,' she defended, her cheeks still red. 'I haven't drunk alcohol since I found out it puts me flat on my back.' She drew in an angry breath at his knowing look. 'I meant it makes me lose consciousness! After it happened to me the first couple of times I went to a doctor and he told me my body just won't accept alcohol.'

'I would say that's a pretty shrewd analysis,' Caleb Steele mocked arrogantly.

She glared at him. 'You needn't sound so damned disapproving,' she snapped. 'You were the one that took an unconscious woman to bed!' She gasped once she had made the accusation, although Caleb Steele didn't move a muscle.

'You responded OK when I touched you,' he drawled uninterestedly.

Her cry of horror was preceded only by the return of the heated colour to her cheeks. She *had* gone to bed with this man, made love with him. Oh God!

Caleb Steele showed little concern for her disturbed state. 'What did you do the last couple of times it happened?' he asked drily, leaning one hip against the dressing-table, completely relaxed, his arms crossed in front of his powerful chest.

Cat's gaze dropped from the bored interest she

could read in his eyes as he waited for her
answer. 'I was with friends——'

'And this time you weren't.' He straightened,
the casual movement causing Cat to press back
against the pillows, the sudden gleam in those
fathomless black eyes mocking her nervousness.
'This time the little cat was left amongst the
wolves!' he scorned contemptuously.

Wolf! She would lay odds on this man being
the only wolf at the party last night, for all that it
had turned out to be a little wild; and now that he
had had her he was spitting her out again!

His eyes narrowed on her flushed face. 'You
aren't one of Luke's college friends, are you?' He
sounded as if that thought didn't please him at all.

'No, I——' She broke off, the real reason she
had gone to the party the previous evening, the
remembered wish to make a good impression on
this man, still paramount. She couldn't blurt it all
out now, not when she had just spent the night
with him. 'I'm just an acquaintance, really,' she
amended.

He gave a slow nod. 'And do you usually look
this good in the mornings?'

She gazed back at him in alarm. Surely he
hadn't changed his mind and was now in the
mood to repeat what had happened between them
last night? She clutched the sheet even tighter to
her.

'Relax, Cat,' he drawled, the amusement back
in his eyes, even if his mouth only showed a
cynical twist. 'I was referring to the fact that most
women I know can't wait to run to the mascara
bottle in the mornings.'

Most women he knew! She would bet that amounted to several hundred. Caleb Steele was known for the short and not always sweet affairs he had had since his divorce from his wife fifteen years ago. Any of those women showing the least sign of wanting permanence in his life was out like an old pair of shoes. Any women that tried to take on this man, even temporarily, was a braver one than she!

'You have naturally black lashes, hmm?' he mused as she made no answer.

'No,' she denied abruptly. 'I have them dyed.'

'You do?' He didn't even bother to try to hide his surprise.

She nodded, all the time conscious of that reflected image above her, hating the mirrors, feeling as if she had no place to hide. 'At the hairdressers,' she supplied. 'It's done all the time,' she claimed at his cynical expression.

'I know that,' he derided, shaking his head in disgust. 'I just didn't think you—there soon won't be many parts of a woman's body that are completely natural!' he rasped.

His scorn irritated her. 'The rest of me is real!' she snapped. 'Although what you said earlier isn't true; my body is far from perfect. My legs are too long for one thing——'

'I wouldn't know,' he mocked. 'I'm a breast man myself. And yours are a pair of the finest I've ever seen. Not too big, but not too small either, with a dusky rose nip——'

'Please!' she groaned her dismay at his familiarity with her body.

'Oh I did.' He moved forward with a feline

grace, sitting down on the bed, one arm resting on the bed across her, the other beside her. 'Do you have any idea of the pleasure a man can get from the taste of your breasts, the soft little moans you give in your throat as your nipples are kissed and caressed to——'

'Please!' He was making her feel giddy, his proximity alarming, what he was saying even more so, a mental picture of them the way he was describing burning in her brain, able to imagine his dark head bent over her as he sipped from those life-giving peaks, as she cradled him to her and——

'Yes, Cat.' His black gaze held hers as he gently released the sheet from her suddenly relaxed fingers, as he softly pulled the sheet down to throw it back on the floor, leaving Cat's naked body exposed to him in all its silken glory. 'It was just like that,' he murmured huskily as his head slowly lowered and that hard mouth claimed one taut nipple with surprising softness and warmth, the rough rasp of his tongue sending aching pleasure down between her thighs.

Her head fell back, and as it did so she could see him in the mirror above exactly as she had imagined him, her skin creamy white in contrast to his black hair, her hand moving up even now so that her fingers could entwine in his hair as she held him against her, groaning anew as he moved to claim the other dusky nipple, drinking his fill of that one, too, Cat unable to look away from the beauty of their reflections above.

'Dad, I—bloody hell!'

The shocked English-accented voice of this

man's son as he burst into the room unannounced was what brought her back to her senses, gasping her dismay at what had happened, and at the identity of the intruder to their pleasure. Caleb Steele's *son*. Oh God, she groaned for what must have been the dozenth time since waking up to find herself in this man's bed.

Caleb slowly eased himself back, holding her horrified gaze with steady intensity. 'Get out of here, Luke,' he instructed coldly, not even turning to look at his son.

'But, Dad——'

'I said get out!' He didn't raise his voice, and he still didn't turn towards the door as his body partly shielded Cat's, but the icy anger was obvious in the tersely spoken order, every muscle in his body tensed in challenge of his authority. 'We'll talk about this later.' There was a threat rather than apology in his voice.

'OK,' Luke Steele sighed, the soft click of the door telling them he had obeyed the first instruction, too.

Cat's eyes were squeezed tightly shut as she denied the reflection of her nakedness, not in the mirrors this time, but in coal-black depths. Caleb Steele's eyes. She didn't know what had possessed her, what had possessed *him*; she wasn't exactly his usual type. She was too young to be one of his women; he had publicly stated on more than one occasion that any woman under thirty didn't have the experience or maturity he liked. Surely at twenty-four she was too young!

What was she doing lying here assuring herself she was too young for him? She had just spent the night with him, had been lost in his arms again seconds ago when his son burst in.

She felt the bed ease beside her as he stood up, the gentle caress of the silk sheet as it was placed over her. But still her eyes remained squeezed shut.

'It's all right, Cat.' That silky rough voice spoke softly. 'He's gone now.'

She moistened her lips, lying rigidly still, feeling his presence as he stood beside the bed looking down at her, even though she couldn't see him!

'But I haven't, hmm?' Caleb read her mind. 'Isn't it a little late to feel embarrassment in front of me?' he derided.

It was that amusement in his voice that made her lids fly open, and she turned to glare at him. 'I'm sure that you're used to waking up in bed next to a different woman every day of the week,' she snapped. 'But I'm not used to this at all!'

He wasn't in the least moved by her show of temper. 'Every day of the week sounds a little excessive,' he drawled mockingly. 'Even I like to rest on Sundays.'

God, why was she even bothering to talk to this man when all she wanted to do was to get dressed and get out of here—or did she mean crawl out of here? She had arrived with such plans the night before, had hoped to get the information she needed; now she knew she would have to start all over again. She doubted Caleb Steele would appreciate her request when she had literally fallen into bed with him; it smacked too much like payment for the night! She might write what most people would consider 'lightweight' stuff but she took her job seriously, and trying in any way to influence a person to give her information was not the way she worked. She realised that after last night she would have to work doubly hard to convince Caleb Steele of that.

She sat up, holding the sheet to her. 'Then as this is a Sunday I'm sure you would like to begin doing that,' she encouraged firmly.

Black brows arched. 'Would you be ordering me out of my own bedroom?'

'I would be—asking you to think about it,' she grimaced.

The stern mouth actually quirked this time, although he didn't show his teeth in a smile. Perhaps he never did actually smile or laugh; any photographs she had seen of him had always shown him grim-faced. She had assumed that to be because he considered the photographer to be infringing on his privacy. Now she wasn't so sure.

'I've thought about it,' he derided. 'I'm quite happy where I am for the moment.'

'I—your breakfast,' she reminded a little desperately, not at all happy with 'where he was'.

He gave an inclination of his head. 'I've changed my mind about that. I think I'll order us something in here while you take a shower.'

Cat swallowed hard, judging the distance between the bed and the bathroom door. It was too far! Wide green eyes turned back to him, and she was sure they were panic-stricken.

He looked a little impatient with this display of

modesty. 'Take the sheet with you,' he advised
wearily.

'Take the—oh. Yes.' Her expression cleared.

But wrapping a sheet around herself that was
both way too big and extremely slippery proved
much more difficult than she had anticipated. It
always seemed to be so elegantly done in films
and on television, but after several minutes she
still hadn't managed to get the sheet about her
with any degree of safety.

'Here.' Caleb Steele finally took pity on her
struggles, draping the loose sheet over her free
arm while securing the end of it between her
breasts. 'Relax,' he instructed drily without
looking up from his task as she flinched at the
intimacy. 'Don't you know that this sort of
modesty is a thing of the past? It's very well
done, though,' he drawled, stepping back to look
at her with dispassionate eyes. 'Maybe I could
find a part for you. Did you have anything in
mind?'

'In mind?' She was standing now, aware that
she barely reached this man's shoulder in her
bare feet, also aware that the two-inch heels on
her shoes wouldn't make that much difference
either.

He pulled a face. 'The casting-couch may be
long dead, but the bed isn't.' He gave the latter a
derisive look, its tumbled look showing evidence
of their presence there together.

Cat swallowed hard. 'You think—that is—
you believe——'

He once again crossed his arms in front of his
powerful chest. 'Did the director prove difficult?'

he mocked. 'If it was Maurice Goodson I'm not surprised.' His mouth twisted. 'He's a happily married man and never touches other women.'

'I'm glad to hear it,' she bit out tautly. 'Maybe some of his scruples will rub off on you——'

'I'm not married,' he told her coldly. 'And not intending to be.' He studied her between narrowed lids. 'So if that's the role you're after, kid, forget it.'

She didn't know whether she was more angry at being called 'kid' or at the way he assumed she had gone to bed with him because she had in mind being the next Mrs Caleb Steele. She decided the latter more urgently needed rebuttal. 'You flatter yourself if you think I would even consider marrying someone as cold and arrogant as you,' she dismissed hardly. 'And contrary to what you think there's more to life, *my* life, than using people for gain. The real world isn't like that!'

'The real world is exactly like that,' he derided pityingly.

'Not my world,' she insisted. 'I don't want anything from you, Mr Steele. Whatever happened between us last night was not planned. I don't want payment, in any way, shape, or form for it. You——'

'You know,' he remarked softly, almost conversationally, 'it's as well we didn't get to do too much talking last night; I can't stand women that nag.'

'You—you——'

'Go take your shower, Cat,' he dismissed in a bored voice. 'And take this with you.'

'This' was the shimmering green dress she had worn the evening before and which he had just picked up from the bedroom floor, reminding her more forcefully than anything else could have done that she had casually spent the night with this man. She felt as if *she* didn't know herself any more, so why should Caleb Steele!

She snatched the dress from his hand, looking around for the lace panties that were all she had worn beneath the clinging material, her cheeks colouring anew as she saw Caleb Steele was holding those out to her, too. They were really just the minutest scrap of pale green lace, and she crushed it within her hand.

'We'll talk as soon as you've had your shower,' he told her confidently, picking up the telephone at the end of the statement, talking crisply into the receiver as he ordered a full breakfast for both of them.

Cat hastily shut the bathroom door before his talk of grilled food made her physically ill. How could this have happened to her? She had come to the party last night in all innocence. Admittedly it was a little wilder than she had anticipated, the majority of the guests appearing to be around the nineteen or twenty mark as their young host was. She hadn't particularly liked that cynical young man from the beginning, and she had a fair idea that he had been the one who had doctored her drinks, seeming to dislike her as much as she disliked him. When his father had appeared on the scene she didn't know, but he obviously had, and with the alcohol in her system she had gone to bed with him. Which was very strange, because usually she just passed out!

She didn't believe she had made love with Caleb Steele, no matter what he said to the contrary!

She turned straight round and marched back into the bedroom, no longer caring that she wore only the draped sheet. 'You're a lying, rotten, lousy——' She broke off as she realised Caleb Steele was no longer alone, that an older man had joined him, a well-dressed pleasant-faced man who appeared to be taking instructions when she entered the room. And from the cursory glance he gave in her direction, the blue eyes completely devoid of emotion, he found nothing unusual in seeing a sheet-wrapped woman walking about his employer's bedroom suite!

Black eyes met her stormy green ones with icy disdain. And then Caleb Steele turned away and resumed his business discussion with the man at his side.

Cat couldn't believe it, had never been dismissed in such a way before! It was just as if she were of no importance at all. She drew in an angry breath. 'I said——'

'I heard you.' His head snapped up. 'It may have escaped your notice,' he drawled with heavy sarcasm, 'but I'm busy right now.'

Busy! *He* was busy. She was trying to regain her self-respect and he was busy! It may be clichéd, but who the hell did he think he was! The answer to that was all too obvious, but who he was and the amount of money he was worth, didn't much matter to her at this moment. Who *she* was, and the amount of money she *wasn't* worth didn't mean Caleb Steele could dismiss her like an old shirt! If he treated all of his women in this way it was no wonder his affairs didn't last.

'You may be busy, Mr Steele——' her chin rose challengingly when his associate at last showed surprise—at her formality with the man who's bedroom she stood almost naked in. It was the erroneous impression her appearance gave that made her carry on in spite of the cold anger emitting from Caleb Steele. 'But I want to talk to you. Now,' she added firmly as she guessed he was about to dismiss her a second time. 'Unless you would care to discuss what happened in that bed last night in front of an audience?'

The man at his side gave a choked sound, somewhere between a cough and a laugh, beginning to cough in earnest as that coal-black gaze was suddenly riveted on him.

'You sound bad, Norm,' his employer grated with icy insincerity. 'Why don't you go and get yourself a cup of coffee and we'll continue with this later. When you're feeling better.' The last was added threateningly.

'Sure.' The other man spoke for the first time, American like his employer. 'I—er—nice to have met you, Miss—er——'

'Cat,' Caleb Steele put in icily before she could make any reply. 'And believe me,' he drawled suggestively, 'she more than lives up to her name!' He flexed his shoulders as if something there pained him.

Like claw marks, from a *cat!* And she knew

damn well that except for that fine covering of dark hair his back was smooth and unmarked.

A speculative light entered the man Norm's eyes. 'Perhaps we'll meet again, Cat,' he murmured in a somewhat puzzled voice, as if for once he were surprised at his employer's choice of a bed-partner.

'I doubt that,' she answered him but looked at Caleb Steele. 'I wound to kill!'

'Yes. Well,' the older man looked flustered now, 'I'll talk to you later, Caleb.' He made a hasty exit before he was caught in the verbal war that seemed to be taking place in the bedroom.

Caleb Steele looked at her with expressionless black eyes. 'And just how do you intend to wound me, Catherine Howard?' he challenged in a softly threatening voice.

Her eyes flashed. 'If I had any sense I'd stab you in the back the way my namesake should have done Henry the Eighth! You're as lying and deceitful as he ever was!' She tossed back her mane of golden hair.

'I am?'

Steel encased in velvet. There was no other way to describe that softly spoken threat. But she wasn't about to be intimidated by him; he had lied to her and he was going to admit it. 'I didn't make love with you in that bed,' she pointed to it angrily. 'Or anywhere else last night!'

Dark brows rose. 'You didn't?' he drawled.

'You know I didn't.' Her eyes flashed. 'I always pass out. I don't—don't——'

'Leap into bed with men you don't know,' he finished coldly. 'Then how did you wake up in my bed this morning?'

Delicate colour darkened her cheeks. 'I don't believe you slept in it. I also don't remember you being at the party last night. I can't remember seeing you there, and——'

'I arrived late,' he bit out, as if he were tired of the whole conversation. 'And I did sleep in that bed last night. Next to you.'

She swallowed hard, knowing by the flat uninterested tone of his voice that he didn't lie. But she *always* passed out!

Her distress must have shown in her face, because something like compassion flickered in his eyes. 'Cat——'

'I'm sorry,' she bit out jerkily, swinging away, needing to escape back to the sanctuary of the bathroom. 'I was rude to you just now in front of an employee.' She couldn't think straight, needed to be alone away from the tumbled intimacy of this bedroom so that she could try to piece together the events of last night, try to make some sense of it in her own mind. 'I—I'll apologise later if you would like me to. I—I'll go and take my shower now——'

'Cat!'

Again she ignored the steely command in his voice, running into the bathroom, locking the door behind her this time before collapsing back against it.

If only she could remember, if only she knew what had happened last night to make her want to make love to Caleb Steele. She couldn't believe she *had* wanted to make love with him; she didn't even like the man.

What had Vikki said to her before she left for

the party last night, 'Be good'? And then they had both come back with the rejoinder about 'being careful' before Cat had laughingly taken her leave. She had no idea whether she had been 'good', but careful she certainly hadn't been.

How could she have taken Caleb Steele as her lover when she belonged heart and soul to Harry?

CHAPTER TWO

SHE had been so buoyed up the evening before as she got ready for the party, overjoyed at the prospect of finally meeting Caleb Steele after weeks of writing for an interview to his London office and home when her publisher had told her he was the only way she would ever be able to speak to his father, the reclusive author Lucien Steele.

The series of articles she had done the year before on Hollywood marriages had proved to be a tremendous success, a publishing company approaching her about doing a book on the subject, with the condition that she covered four marriages of their choice, the rest being left to her discretion. Unfortunately, one of the marriages the publishing company had chosen had been that of Lucien Steele and the late Sonia Harrison. Of course, Cat could have gone ahead and written the chapter on this golden couple of the Hollywood of the forties without talking to Lucien Steele, but she hadn't wanted to do that. But to actually arrange an interview with him had proved more difficult than she had imagined, the now elderly man having disappeared from the Hollywood scene thirty years ago after the tragic death of his wife in a fire that had destroyed their mansion house, and absenting himself from London society a few years ago, too, to all intents and purposes disappearing off the face of the earth. Except that his son and grandson *had* to know of his whereabouts.

She had been warned of Caleb Steele's aversion to meeting the press whenever possible but she hadn't realised he could be so elusive, almost as bad as his father. Polite letters to his office had been ignored; telephone requests to have a meeting with Caleb Steele had been politely evaded by his secretary; a visit to his London home two days ago had introduced her to Luke Steele, his notorious son. Where the grandfather and father seemed to avoid publicity the grandson seemed to court it! He was always in trouble of one kind or another, always being asked to leave hotels and restaurants because of his outrageous behaviour, and had been thrown out of two universities at the last count.

But he had been very friendly towards her yesterday afternoon, and if she had been a little wary of his over-bright eyes and unkempt appearance she forgave him the minute he invited her to his party, assuring her that his father was going to be there.

She had even ignored the over-familiarity and the provocative remarks he kept making when she got to the party, and the way it seemed impossible to escape his company—or not to notice the amount of alcohol he was consuming.

She could remember all that, the noise, the loud laughter of too many people having drunk too much, could remember deciding shortly before eleven that Caleb Steele wasn't going to come to his son's party after all, remembered

telling Luke Steele she was leaving, and then—
nothing. The next thing she had been aware of
was that slap to her bottom!

Promiscuity hadn't been something she consciously avoided, but something she ignored.
That sort of relationship was for other people,
not her. She had her friends, a lot of them, male
and female alike, admittedly more of the latter
than the former, but that was probably because a
lot of men didn't believe there could be just
friendship between a man and a woman. She
believed the opposite, that friendship should
come before the love. She and Harry had been
friends from the moment they walked through
the gate on their first day at school, when Harry
had given a painful tug on the single braid that
lay down her spine, and she had turned around
and punched him straight on the nose! They had
both been too proud to cry and so they had
laughed instead. After that they had be come
inseparable, their friendship surprising them
both—if not other people—by turning to love
when they were both fifteen.

And she had betrayed that love last night with
a man like Caleb Steele!

She didn't even need to guess what Harry
would think of the other man; she knew the two
men would have disliked each other intensely,
Harry so open and boyishly handsome, Caleb
Steele hiding any emotions he might have behind
that harsh face and cold black eyes. They were as
different as night and day, one devil, one angel,
and she—she had lain with the devil!

A brisk knock on the bathroom door made

her jump nervously. 'Breakfast is here, Cat,' Caleb Steele informed her abruptly. 'Either run the water and have a shower or come out and eat,' he advised irritably. 'You can't stay in there all day.'

She wished she could! Maybe other women could handle this situation confidently, but she couldn't. And she certainly couldn't sit down to breakfast in an evening dress!

'Cat?' his voice had sharpened. 'Have you fallen asleep in there?'

Asleep? She didn't think she was ever going to fall asleep again—too afraid of what she would find when she woke up!

'Answer me, Cat,' he advised in a steely voice. 'Or would you rather suffer the embarrassment of my having someone break the door down?'

She swallowed hard, barely breathing, trembling like a leaf about to fall from a tree. 'I don't want any breakfast,' she told him a quivery voice, on the verge of tears.

'Cat?'

That velvet rasp sounded directly through the wood behind her head, and she moved hastily away, turning to stare at the door with wide eyes.

'Cat, are you crying?' He sounded incredulous at the idea.

Was she crying? Yes, she could taste the tears on her top lip, although she hadn't been aware of them falling. Why shouldn't she cry when her heart was breaking into little pieces!

'Cat, open the door,' he encouraged now, persuasively. 'There's no need for this, Cat,' he cajoled softly. 'Would it help if I told you

nothing happened between us last night? That I
didn't even touch you until this morning?'

Hope flared in her over-bright green eyes, and
then it faded, leaving her looking more miserable
than ever. 'Not when it isn't the truth,' she said
dully.

'But it is,' he insisted firmly. 'I was damned
angry this morning when I let you think we had
made love. Open the door, Cat, and we'll talk.'

Why on earth was he so obsessed with her
unlocking the door? What did he—no, he
couldn't think *that!* God, if she were the type to
commit suicide she would have done it years ago,
and over a much more worthwhile man than
Caleb Steele.

She straightened, her head back proudly. 'I'll
be out as soon as I've showered. Would you
please order me a taxi so that I can leave
immediately?'

For a moment that was silence on the other
side of the door. 'Very well,' he bit out coldly, no
longer so close to the door. 'The hysterics are
over, I take it? he derided.

She stiffened. 'You can rest assured that I don't
intend using your razor to cut my wrists!'

'That might be a little difficult,' he drawled. 'I
use an electric shaver!'

Cat bristled indignantly at his mockery. 'I
could always used it as a saw!'

A soft throaty chuckle answered her anger.
'Your name *does* fit, Cat,' he murmured admiringly. 'You spit and claw right back, don't you?'

'I thought you already knew that,' she
reminded bitterly.

'I told you,' he said softly. 'I didn't make love to you last night.'

Was he telling the truth? She didn't know. But she desperately *needed* to believe that he was, slowly unlocking and opening the door, looking up at him anxiously, coal-black eyes staring straight back at her. And she could read nothing from them, years of deliberately shielding his emotions making that impossible. Cat continued to stare back at him.

'You were already in my bed when I got home,' Caleb Steele told her briskly. 'And by that time I was too damned tired to care *who* I shared my bed with!'

Cat's face drained of colour, leaving two deep green pools of bewildered hurt.

'How the hell old are you that it shocks you out of your mind to even *think* of sharing a bed with a man?' He scowled at the accusation in her expression.

'Old enough,' she muttered.

'For what?' He turned away disgustedly, his hands thrust into the pockets of his trousers, pulling the material taut across his thighs.

'For whatever,' she returned sharply.

'Eighteen isn't old enough for whatever!' he rasped, scowling heavily. 'Is there anyone that's going to be worried by your non-appearance last night?' he suddenly frowned.

She thought of Vikki, and then as quickly dismissed her friend and flatmate. Vikki would probably be gleefully lying in wait for her when she got home, demanding to know all the details, had been urging her for years to take a lover.

'You mean like a father or brother?' She arched honey-blonde brows at him.

His mouth was tight. 'Or a husband?'

Her laugh was brittle. 'God, yes, I could be married, couldn't I?' she said hardly.

'Are you?' Black eyes were narrowed, as if he didn't like the idea of sharing a bed with a married woman, under any circumstances.

'No,' she assured him flatly. 'Nor engaged, nor seeing anyone seriously. I don't have a brother and my parents live in Cornwall, so you needn't worry about Daddy coming after you with a shotgun!'

'Is that a possibility?' Caleb Steele asked slowly.

'Not if it's true that we didn't make love.' There was a question in the statement.

'And if it isn't true?' he grated.

She shrugged. 'Then my father is old-fashioned enough to want his grandchild to have a father. But you were telling the truth when you said we didn't make love, weren't you?' Anxiety darkened her eyes, although her expression remained bland.

He considered her for long, timeless minutes before nodding abruptly. 'I'd been in a meeting for over forty-eight hours; I have union trouble.' There was a resigned twist to his mouth. 'But yesterday was Luke's birthday——'

'It was?' Cat gasped; it hadn't been like any other birthday party she had ever gone to!

'It was,' he nodded, giving an impatient sigh as he watched her continually hitch the sheet over her breasts in an effort to keep it in place, turning with leashed energy to push open one of the mirrored doors to his wall-length wardrobe, searching inside.

'Do you have a mirror fetish?' Cat burst out impetuously, fascinated by the way there were mirrors everywhere, even on two walls in the adjoining bathroom; it had come as something of a shock to see the tousled reflection of herself across the width of the luxurious room, the sunken jacuzzi meaning she had an unhindered full-length view of herself!

He turned briefly to give her a dismissive glance. 'If you're expecting me to say they were already in the house when I moved in you're going to be disappointed,' he drawled, taking out a dark brown robe. 'Here, put this on.' He held it out to her.

She gratefully took the robe, then looked down awkwardly at the sheet, wondering how she was going to go from one to the other and still maintain her modesty.

'Let's not go through that again,' Caleb Steele whipped the sheet from around her body, holding out the robe for her to put her arms into. 'You were naked when I climbed into bed next to you last night, and you didn't even have the sheet on you when I woke up this morning!' he dismissed impatiently.

'That isn't the point,' a red-faced Cat snapped, quickly turning to put her arms into the robe.

'Because you're awake now?' he mocked. 'There,' he murmured softly. '*That's* why I like mirrors.'

She froze, slowly turning her head to look at

him, but he was staring up at the ceiling, and
with the heated colour darkening her cheeks she
reluctantly followed his gaze.

She had her arms thrust into the sleeves of the
robe but he hadn't yet put the material in place
about her shoulders, her back arched, her breasts
thrust out invitingly. The reflection reminded
her all too forcibly that earlier she had issued a
similar invitation—and that he had accepted!

She pulled the robe about her in hurried
movements, her cheeks burning as she tied the
belt about her slender waist, the thigh-length
robe reaching down past her knees, the sleeves
falling down over her hands as she straightened
her arms.

'Let me.' Caleb Steele moved to turn up the
sleeves, treating her with all the resigned patience
of an adult dealing with a recalcitrant child. 'I
could snap you in half and not even know I'd
done it,' he murmured as if to himself.

'*I'd* know you had done it,' she told him with
feeling.

The coal-black eyes became even darker, the
cynical light going out of them to be replaced by
a surprising warmth, before that stern mouth
actually curved into a grin, deep grooves etched
into his cheeks, his teeth very white against his
tanned flesh.

Cat's eyes widened like a surprised feline.
'Why do you hide all that dental work?' she once
again spoke without thinking first. 'I mean, you
rarely smile,' she tried to amend, grimacing her
embarrassment as she knew she had failed.

This time he laughed outright, a rich deep

sound, roughness once again cloaked in velvet. 'Like everyone else I laugh when something amuses me.' He still smiled. 'And I'll have you know that these teeth are all my own, and they're the genuine uncapped variety!'

She stared at him in fascination, amazed at the difference his smile made. He looked almost handsome! And years younger, not quite so much as if every minute of his thirty-nine years had been spent amassing the power and money that made him the dangerous man he was.

'Cat?'

She suddenly realised he was no longer smiling, but eyeing her watchfully as she openly stared at him. 'I can see that now,' she rushed into speech. 'One of the front ones is a little crooked.'

He nodded. 'If you were a guest at my son's party last night why didn't you know it was his nineteenth birthday?' he asked icily.

This man would have been lethal as a court-room lawyer, would have held the judge and jury mesmerised by the way he never missed even the slightest irregularity!

'He didn't tell me,' she answered truthfully.

'If you're a friend——'

'I told you, I'm only an acquaintance.' She bit her lip. 'I—I went to the party last night because I wanted to meet you,' she revealed, knowing honesty had to prevail now.

His eyes glazed over, his nostrils flaring, his mouth a thin angry line. 'So it *was* all an act,' he said disgustedly. 'The surprise, the dismay, the *shock*,' he added impatiently. 'When I didn't show at the party you decided to wait for me, in my bed!' He began to pace the room, shaking his head as he looked at her. 'You ought to get an Oscar for the act you just put on in the bathroom,' he grated. 'I actually did feel a first-class heel for lying to you!'

'Because you are!' Her eyes flashed. 'It was cruel to make me believe we had—we had been lovers. Everything I told you was the truth, my drinks were doctored, and I have no idea how I came to be in your bed——'

'For God's sake don't start crying again!' he rasped as the tears began to fall. 'We'll get to the bottom of this once and for all,' he bit out, picking up the receiver to dial. 'Luke?' he barked in the mouthpiece. 'Get in here,' he ordered as coldly as he had earlier told his son to leave. 'And make sure your story is a good one!' he advised threateningly before slamming down the receiver to once again pace the room.

For all the notice he took of Cat as they waited for the arrival of his son she might as well not have been here.

'Do you always talk to him that way?' she finally asked curiously.

His head snapped back, his hands thrust into his trouser pockets again. 'What way?'

She shrugged. 'Like one of the hired help,' she frowned.

His mouth twisted. 'If I spoke to Norm in that way he would leave.'

'Your son doesn't have the same prerogative,' she drawled.

'But he does,' Caleb Steele corrected in a hard voice. 'He's his own man.'

Man sounded a little hopeful for the immature boy she had witnessed at the party last night, his youth obvious in the way he drank too much, laughed too loud, and was too familiar with a woman five years his senior. She doubted Caleb Steele had ever been *that* young, had been married and on his way to becoming a father at the same age.

'Let me put that another way,' he drawled, seeming to guess her thoughts. 'Luke is independently wealthy from money given to him by his mother, and at nineteen he's over the age of consent.' He shrugged broad shoulders. 'If he doesn't like the way I talk to him he's free to set up on his own.'

The underlying friction of the father towards his son was unmistakable. But considering the amount of newsworthy trouble Luke Steele had been in over the last couple of years perhaps that was understandable. She had found the younger man to be totally brash and rude. And, secretly, she couldn't forgive his witnessing those moments of intimacy she had shared with his father earlier!

'Don't look so worried, little cat,' Caleb murmured throatily. 'We won't come to blows over you.'

If they did she had no doubt who would be the victor. And she had a feeling Caleb Steele didn't either, despite the fact that he was twice his son's age. She also knew he didn't give a damn how she felt, that he once again believed the worst of her.

'Do you get a lot of women throwing themselves at you?' she frowned.

Black eyes narrowed to steely slits. 'I've never

actually had a woman I don't know waiting for me in my own bed before,' he bit out.

'I——'

'Come in, Luke,' he called out to his son as a knock sounded on the door.

Physically father and son were very alike, although Luke's eyes were a deep blue. They both possessed that rugged attraction rather than handsomeness, but maturity had given Caleb that cynical light in his eyes where Luke displayed only recklessness. And in contrast to Caleb's tailored shirt and trousers Luke looked the height of casualness in faded denims and a loose sweater. The bravado in his stance was directed at both his father and Cat.

He nodded in recognition of her, his insolence barely contained. 'Miss Howard,' he drawled. 'So nice of you to have stayed the night.' In contrast to his father's American drawl his English accent sounded very precise—and insulting.

Cat knew that after the break-up of his father's marriage the boy had gone to live with his grandfather before being sent to school in England. The fact that the two even spoke with a different accent made them even less like father and son.

'Did I have any choice?' she returned tartly.

He gave a careless shrug. 'You didn't look as if you wanted one earlier.'

Colour heightened her cheeks. 'You——'

'Luke, what the hell is going on?' His father's voice cracked between them like a whip. 'Do you know anything about Cat being in my bed?'

Luke shrugged again. 'Only what I saw this morning——'

'You know a lot more than——'

'Cat, I'm trying to find out what happened,' Caleb cut in coldly.

'Well you won't do that from your son,' she snapped, glaring at the younger man.

'Luke will tell me the truth.' His voice brooked no argument—or deception.

'I wish I had your faith,' she muttered. 'So far, in our very *short* acquaintance, your son has shown himself to be anything but truthful!' she challenged.

Luke Steele didn't even blink an eyelid. 'I would doubt you have been completely honest with my father either,' he sounded confident. 'Otherwise there would be no need for this conversation.'

Cat shot him a resentful glare. 'I have told your father everything I know about last night. Unfortunately, he doesn't believe me,' she added disgustedly.

'Maybe you would like to tell me what you know, Luke.' It was phrased as an invitation, but there was no doubt in anyone's mind that it was an order.

'I think there's only one thing about Miss Howard that you will really be interested in.' Luke spoke again in that confident voice, as if, despite everything, he was sure he had the upper hand.

Cat tensed warily, sensing danger.

'Oh?' his father prompted guardedly.

'Cat is a reporter,' Luke announced in a bored voice. 'The one that's been asking to be introduced to Grandpop the last three months.'

If Cat had thought Caleb Steele's eyes were chilly before then she learnt a new meaning to the word at that moment, the black orbs as hard as pebbles and cold as ice! Luke was right, knowing she was a reporter did seem to be the only thing his father was interested in now.

'You're *that* C. Howard?' he bit out with icy accusation.

He made her sound—and feel—like some sort of low life that had accidentally wandered into his pampered world, as if just being in the same room with her contaminated him!

He turned furious eyes on his son. 'If you knew who she was, what was she doing at your party?'

Luke looked taken aback by the attack, as if he had expected that little fact to be overlooked by his father's anger at finding her here at all. 'I—well—she's been making a pest of herself, and so I thought——'

'I haven't been making a pest of myself,' she disclaimed indignantly. 'All of my letters to this family have been polite, the telephone calls, too.'

'All twenty-one of them,' Caleb Steele acknowledged in a hard voice. 'Oh yes,' he confirmed softly at her startled look. 'I'm well aware of the amount of times you've called, and the reason for them.'

'Then——'

'And you must be aware that they could be called harassment,' he added coldly.

'Nothing of the sort,' she dismissed impatiently. 'I always took no for an answer, and it was the only way I could contact you when you refused to even acknowledge my letters.'

'The mere fact that I didn't acknowledge them should have been answer enough!'

She had known that, of course; she would have had to have been patently insensitive not to have done! But she wasn't the type of reporter that liked to write because of someone else's unhappiness or misfortune. She had discovered that long ago, and she never sent anything to print without first talking to the people involved, and also getting their OK on what she had written before sending it in. There was already too much misery in the world without having it constantly emblazoned across the front page of newspapers. Faint-hearted, some of her colleagues had called her in the early days, but she had felt comforted by the fact that she did at least have a heart of some sort! And that was the reason she couldn't in all conscience do the chapter in her book on Lucien Steele and his wife without talking to him first.

'I only wanted to meet your father, talk to him for a while,' she pleaded her case. 'I told you, I'm writing a book——'

'My mother has been dead nearly thirty years,' Caleb Steele scorned. 'Most people today haven't even heard of her, let alone that she was married to Lucien Steele!'

'You know that isn't true,' she protested at that blatant lie about Sonia Harrison, one of the screen-goddesses of the forties and fifties. 'They had a season of her films on only last summer!'

He sighed, his gaze steely. 'She's still old news,' he dismissed.

'My publisher doesn't happen to think so.' She shook her head.

'So write your book,' he invited harshly. 'You don't need my permission to do that. But make sure you only write the facts, because as soon as the book is published I intend to have my lawyers go over what you've written about my parents with a fine toothcomb!'

She had already guessed that. If only she could make him understand that she had no intention of writing anything defamatory about either of his parents. 'Look, I know that because of the fact that your father is into his seventies now there was a rumour a couple of years ago that he no longer writes his own books, but——'

A harsh laugh interrupted her. 'My father is more lucid at seventy-four than a lot of men are at half his age!' Caleb Steele scorned. 'The whole idea was ridiculous from the first.'

She was sure it was. But even if it weren't it was none of her business; she was only interested in the time the now elderly man had been married to Sonia Harrison. 'I wish you would see——'

'Oh, I do, Miss Howard,' he assured her coldly, turning that icy gaze on his son once more. 'I have yet to hear a reasonable explanation from you,' he prompted hardly.

A flush darkened the young boy's cheeks, the expression in his eyes more reckless than ever. 'I thought you should meet Cat,' he shrugged. 'Talk to her. And then maybe she would get lost.'

'She was waiting in my bed for me!' his father snapped disgustedly.

Cat paled. 'I wasn't waiting for you!' She turned glittering eyes on Luke Steele. 'How did I get into your father's bed?' she demanded to know, too angry to mince her words.

'How should I——'

'Don't lie,' she warned with controlled fury. 'The last thing I remember about last night was telling you I was leaving.'

He returned her gaze unblinkingly. 'And the last time I saw you you were on your way out.'

'That's a lie——'

'I don't lie, Cat,' he dismissed in a bored voice.

He was lying now, and she had a fair idea why; his father's anger was formidable, even to this self-confident young man. 'Luke, can't you see you're just making matters worse?' she encouraged. 'You know very well I didn't get as far as leaving the party last night.'

'I know it now,' he nodded.

She gave a frustrated sigh. 'If you're worried about your father's anger then surely you realise he's going to be twice as furious if you don't tell him the truth now?'

Luke gave a harsh laugh, glancing slyly at his father. 'I'm not in the least concerned about Dad's anger,' he scorned. 'What can he do, stop my allowance, throw me out?' He gave a derisive snort.

Caleb looked unmoved by his son's disgraceful behaviour. 'So you aren't telling the truth?' he pounced.

'I didn't say that,' his son drawled dismissively. 'I just don't want Miss Howard to get the impression I'm frightened of you.'

'Aren't you?' his father threatened softly.

Luke blinked, disconcerted for a moment, and then the defiance was back in those restless eyes. 'If that's all?' he derided. 'I'm meeting some friends this morning.'

'Go,' his father dismissed wearily.

With a malicious smile in Cat's direction he did so. Cat disliked him even more than she had yesterday, and with more reason! And yet something about his behaviour struck a chord in her memory.

'They say it's tough being the child of a well-known father,' Caleb Steele mused hardly. 'No one mentions how difficult it is being the father of that child!' He gave a ragged sigh, straightening his shoulders with fresh determination. 'And don't quote me on that,' he rasped warningly.

'I'm not the type——'

'To "kiss and tell"?' he finished scornfully. 'All women are that type, reporters especially so,' he bit out harshly. 'It's a pity you haven't actually experienced my lovemaking so that you can give me a rating as a lover; publicity like that could be very beneficial to my social life!'

From what she had heard his social life didn't need any boosting, women falling over themselves to go out with him! And he obviously held every one of them in contempt for finding him attractive.

'I think you should concentrate on straightening out your son rather than worrying about your social life,' she told him tartly.

He became suddenly still. 'What did you say?'

Steel cloaked in velvet again. She was coming

to know some of the facets of this man's personality, and right now he was furiously angry at her for daring to interfere between him and his son. But she had finally realised what it was about Luke that was so familiar, recognised it and feared it. 'At the moment your son could go either way,' she spoke with quiet intensity. 'He's teetering on the edge of falling down into that abyss of depravity that will totally destroy him, or coming to his senses and carrying on with his life.'

Caleb Steele scowled. 'What the hell are you talking about?' he demanded impatiently.

She gave a ragged sigh, desperate to make him understand how near his son was to losing all reason. 'Luke is going through a trauma of some kind,' she explained, 'and the only way he knows how to deal with it is by going from one deed of recklessness to another. Last night——'

'Let's forget last night,' he rasped. 'There appear to be two schools of thought concerning that.'

She nodded. 'And you naturally choose to believe your son,' she said without rancour.

'Naturally,' he drawled harshly, watching her with narrowed eyes.

Cat shrugged acceptance of his loyalty. 'One of these days your son is going to do something that's going to hurt someone else very badly, and then it's going to be too late to help him.'

'You speak as if from experience,' he probed slowly.

She knew the nightmare of waking up every morning with only feelings of despair, of knowing the day would only get worse not better, of feeling that way and knowing there was nothing she could do to stop it. Luke Steele showed signs of that inner trapped feeling she had carried about with her for over a year, she had seen it there in his eyes when he momentarily let down his guard. She didn't like him, or the things he was doing, but she understood him. Which was surely more than his father did!

'Believe me, Mr Steele,' she ignored the question in his tone, 'if you don't soon stop Luke it could be too late. He's very angry at the world right now and——'

His mouth twisted. 'I thought you didn't know my son very well,' he taunted.

'I don't,' Cat shook her head. 'And I don't want to know him any better either,' she added with feeling. 'But even I can recognise a wounded animal's cry for help.'

Colour darkened his cheeks. 'And I can't, hm?'

'Maybe you're too close to him,' she sighed.

'Or not close enough?' he mocked hardly.

'Maybe,' she acknowledged reluctantly.

His mouth thinned. 'I've never professed to be the perfect father,' he grated. 'Luke and I have lived apart too much for that. But I don't need some damned amateur coming along offering advice,' he glared at her.

'I'm only trying to help——'

'Then don't!'

'No,' she accepted heavily. 'He's your son, you probably know him better than I do.' Although she hadn't been wrong about the utter despair she had briefly glimpsed in Luke Steele's eyes!

'I wonder why that smacks of condescension?' Caleb derided hardly.

A blush darkened her cheeks. 'I'm sorry. I didn't mean——'

'You meant exactly what you said, and how you said it.' He glanced impatiently at his slender wrist-watch. 'Could you hurry up and get dressed?' he urged. 'I'll drop you off at your home on my way out.'

'That won't be necessary,' she refused abruptly.

'It's very necessary.' He gave a humourless quirk of his mouth. 'This time I intend to see you personally escorted off the premises. Just so that there are no mistakes, you understand?' he taunted. 'And I'm afraid that now you won't have time for breakfast before you leave.'

Cat fled to the bathroom, the mention of food once again making her feel ill.

She felt as conspicious as she thought she would as she travelled to her home in the green evening dress, grateful it was a Sunday and still early enough for there not to be too many people about as Caleb Steele halted the black Porsche outside the Victorian house she shared with Vikki.

Black eyes narrowed on the old but well-maintained house. 'You live alone?'

She shook her head. 'With Vikki, an old shoolfriend. It was her parents' house before they died,' she explained, not wanting him to get the wrong idea about how two young women managed to pay the rent on such a house in London, too! He had altogether too bad an opinion of her already, without assuming she was a 'kept woman'! Or worse!

'No father nearby, no brother,' he murmured thoughtfully. 'And no live-in lover.'

'That doesn't make me unusual, Mr Steele,' she snapped.

'I'm well aware of that,' he drawled pointedly.

Colour darkened her cheeks. 'Then why the surprise?'

Black eyes turned on her sharply, pinning her to the spot, 'I'm not surprised, Cat,' he bit out. 'I'm just wondering who the hell Harry is!'

CHAPTER THREE

WHO was Harry? It was a very long time since anyone had asked her that, since anyone had *needed* to ask. Harry had been a fixture in her life for so long that to see one without the other had been cause for speculation. Had been. Harry was gone now.

'Who told you about Harry?' She frowned at Caleb Steele.

He pulled a face. 'Sufficient to say I know about him. So who is he?'

Cat wasn't satisfied with his answer. How did he know about Harry? This man hadn't even realised who *she* was until his son had told him, so how did he just *know* about Harry? 'You just said you knew about him,' she returned guardedly.

His mouth thinned. 'The only thing I know is that you cuddled into me last night and called me Harry!' he rasped.

Cat stared at him with wide, disbelieving eyes, her face crumpling in despair as she saw by his steady, unblinking gaze that he told the truth. 'I'm sorry,' she buried her face in her hands. 'How awful for you . . . I'm so sorry,' she choked again.

'Hey,' a gentle voice finally cajoled, lean fingers gently caressing her damp cheek. 'I've been called worse,' he mocked.

51

Somehow that didn't help, the tears falling all the harder. That she had shared a bed with this man was bad enough, that she had mistaken him for her beloved Harry when she did so was unacceptable.

'Who is he, Cat?' Caleb Steele prompted in a voice that brooked no further delay.

'Was,' she corrected forcefully, her lashes spiky and damp as she looked at him with pained eyes. 'He's dead,' she explained abruptly at his raised brows.

Black eyes narrowed now. 'How long ago?'

'Five years.' She swallowed down the tears. 'He was—killed, the day—the day of our wedding,' she revealed haltingly, knowing this man would persist until he knew it all. And didn't he have that right when she had called him the other man's name! 'It was a beautiful summer's day, the most wonderful day of my life, I thought. But when I arrived at the church my mother told the driver to keep circling, that Harry hadn't arrived yet. I knew there had been a mistake, that Harry wouldn't let me down. I—he was already dead, both he and his best man. Their car went straight under a lorry. They said he was killed outright——'

'Cat, if the police said he was killed instantly then that was what happened,' he cut in firmly.

'They said he felt no pain.' Her eyes were dark and tortured. 'How can they know that?' Her voice was shrill. 'I have nightmares about it, that he was lying there in that twisted hulk of metal that was all that was left of his car, knowing his life's blood was seeping out of him.' Her gaze flew to the harsh face of the man next to her. 'Do you think that he did? Do you think——'

'Cat,' Caleb spoke with cold calm. 'Would it make you feel better to know that he died screaming in agony?'

She gasped at the deliberate cruelty in his voice, and then a tortured breath left her body. 'Thank you,' she squeezed her eyes shut and then opened them again. 'No one has ever spoken that—frankly, before,' she admitted shakily.

'Probably because you've never confided your fears to anyone before.' His dark gaze searched her face. 'Have you?' he prompted.

'No.' It had been easier to talk to a stranger, to someone who wouldn't just offer words of comfort that didn't really mean much because they were only said to make her feel better and not because they were true. 'I don't know why I called you Harry last night——'

'I do,' he bit out harshly. 'You're still in love with him.'

Her head went back as she sensed criticism, her unruly hair long down her spine. 'I'm not ashamed of that,' she defended. 'I've always loved him.'

'But he's——'

'Dead,' she finished harshly. 'Yes, I know. God, how I know,' she added bitterly. 'But death doesn't bring an end to love, not the sort of love I had for Harry.'

'It shouldn't stop your life either,' he told her softly.

'My life hasn't ended,' she told him as one weary of hearing the same advice too many times.

'I work, I have a social life, friends. I even enjoy my life again.' She frowned as she made this admission, knowing that that was exactly what it was, that for over a year after Harry's death she had lived in a state of shock, that when she had finally accepted his death she had had what amounted to a minor nervous breakdown. Then had come the rebuilding of her life so that she could go on. It had been painful and difficult, but she had done it.

And now she was revealing her inner feelings to a man who had believed she would do anything to get a story, including ambushing a man in his own bed! It was the sort of situation she and Harry would have found very amusing in a situation comedy, but when it happened in real life, and to her, it was no longer funny.

'Please talk to your son again,' she requested earnestly. 'I don't care what he said, he isn't telling you the truth about last night.'

Caleb Steele stiffened, the gentle companion of a short time ago completely gone. 'My son doesn't lie to me, Miss Howard,' he rasped.

'Neither do I!' she defended instantly.

His mouth twisted. 'It's unimportant who lied,' he dismissed in a bored voice.

'Not to me it isn't,' she frowned. 'I still want to talk to you about meeting your father.'

He stiffened. 'I don't give interviews. And neither does my father!'

'I don't exactly want to do an interview as such——'

'Just probe into his marriage to my mother,' he bit out. 'Look in the books written about that time, Miss Howard, it's all in there!'

'It couldn't hurt just to talk to him——'

'Doesn't the fact that she died thirty years ago and my father has never remarried tell you that he still loves her?' he snapped. 'That the memory of her, talking about her, still hurts? You, of all people, should understand that,' he accused.

Cat paled. 'I'm sorry.' She gave a confused shake of her head. 'I never thought . . .' God, thirty years and Lucien Steele still hungered for the love he had lost! Would she still feel the desolation of Harry's loss in thirty years? God, it was like a black shadow shrouding her life!

'A reporter's natural instinct,' Caleb Steele derided. 'They never think of the harm or pain they cause, only of the effect the story will have!'

'I'm not like that——'

'Of course you aren't.' His contemptuous expression belied his words.

It was useless arguing with a man who had such a biased opinion of her. If she left it a few days and then contacted him again maybe he would be more receptive. Although she doubted it!

'Thank you for driving me home, Mr Steele,' she said with a politeness that was inborn in her. 'Even though I realise you had the ulterior motive of seeing me out of your home,' politeness couldn't prevent her adding mockingly. 'Perhaps I could call you and—no,' she grimaced at the look he gave her beneath frowning brows.

'We've said it all,' he agreed drily.

Cat got out of the car, standing on the pavement to watch as he drove away before realising how conspicious she must look standing

here in broad daylight wearing an evening dress
at ten o'clock in the morning!

'I won't ask.' Vikki's eyes widened as a
harassed-looking Cat hurried into the house. 'I'll
get us some coffee—and then I'll ask,' she
announced cheerfully. 'There's some hot water if
you want a bath first,' she added brightly, the
fact that they were always in short supply of hot
water of constant annoyance to them both.

Cat knew her gaze was evasive. 'I've already
had a shower,' she muttered.

Her friend's eyes widened even more, and she
seemed about to launch into those questions now,
before clamping her lips together with tremendous effort. 'A change of clothes then,' she
amended. 'And I'll get the coffee.'

She needed more than a change of clothes to
calm her shattered nerves, sitting down on her
bed in the bedroom next to Vikki's. The house
had four bedrooms in all, but the two women
preferred it to be just the two of them.

She and Harry hadn't looked at anyone else
from the time they were fifteen and realised they
were in love. Always and totally together, Harry
had given her a ring when she was seventeen, and
they had spent the next two years saving and
planning for the life they were going to have
together.

Harry had been so handsome, golden-haired,
blue-eyed, with a wicked sense of humour that
had matched her own. They had been like two
parts of a whole, gently teasing each other about
the colour eyes their children would have when
Cat's were so deep a green and Harry's were so

startling a blue; they had no doubt they would be beautiful golden-haired babies when they were both so fair.

Both being only nineteen when they decided to get married a lot of people had still considered them to be only babies themselves. But there had been no doubts in either of their minds that marriage was right for them, both of their families supporting their decision wholeheartedly.

Harry was always a passionate and eager lover, but with a control that had often frustrated her he had refused to make love to her completely, had claimed that he wanted their wedding night to be something they would both remember. Much as it pained her to do so, her reaction to Harry's caresses always instantaneous, she had accepted that decision, although just a few days before the wedding they had almost forgotten that resolve in a blaze of pre-wedding passion.

God, how many times had she wished that she and Harry had made love that night, that she had at least belonged to him completely just once!

The thought that it might have been Caleb Steele that she gave that night to, filled her with distress and shame, burying her face in her hands as she wished she could remember what had happened between them last night. But it was all a blank. And she didn't know if she could accept Caleb Steele's casual dismissal of intimacy; men just didn't get into bed and sleep next to a woman who was a complete stranger to them! Not in her world they didn't. But Caleb said her world wasn't real. She didn't know what was real and what wasn't any more.

'Hey.' A concerned Vikki came down on her knees in front of her. 'It can't be that bad.'

'Worse,' she choked, shaking her head.

Vikki smiled gently, a beautiful red-head, with snapping blue eyes, a sprinkling of freckles across her nose, and a delightful way of being able to laugh at any and everything. She had been Cat's salvation after Harry's death, the two of them sharing this house since that time, more like sisters than just close friends.

'It's no crime to like a man, to find him attractive, to go home with him,' Vikki chided.

'I didn't,' Cat swallowed hard.

Her friend frowned. 'Then where——?'

'I meant I didn't go home with him,' she explained abruptly. 'I was already there,' she added heavily.

'Already there? But——' Vikki looked even more confused. 'Luke Steele?' she sounded disbelieving. 'I've seen photographs of him; he's very good-looking. But——'

'Totally selfish and egotistical,' Cat shook her head. 'And too young. No, it wasn't him. Oh, Vikki, I don't know what I'm going to do!' she wailed. 'I woke up in bed next to the man and——'

'Next to *who?*' Vikki gasped her frustration.

'Mr Steele,' she dismissed. 'And——'

'*Mr* Steele?' Vikki repeated doubtfully.

'Caleb Steele,' she explained impatiently. 'And he——'

'And you still call him Mr?' Vikki frowned her disbelief.

'If you'll listen I'll tell you!' she snapped. 'His son put alcohol in my orange juice——'

'Uh-oh,' her friend grimaced.

'Yes,' she sighed. 'He says he didn't but—Vikki, what usually happens when I pass out?'

'I'm not sure I understand what you mean?' Vikki looked more confused than ever.

'What I mean is, do I do anything, before or after—or during?' she grimaced as she got to what she was really trying to say.

Her friend's brow cleared. 'Unconscious women do not make love with strange men,' she told her confidently.

'But that's just it, Vikki,' she groaned. 'Do I stay unconscious or do I——?'

'Get up on tables and dance naked?' her friend taunted.

'Vikki!'

'Well surely *he* knows whether or not you made love. He wasn't drunk, too, was he?'

'Doubtful,' she said drily, sure Caleb Steele never lost hours out of his life because of drink. 'And he says we didn't make love,' she frowned.

Vikki gave her strained face a considering look. 'But you don't believe him,' she realised.

'It isn't that,' she groaned. 'I—something happened, and—well, it gave me a sense of *déjà vu*.' Colour darkened her cheeks as she recalled watching Caleb in the mirrors above them as he made love to her. At that moment his lovemaking had seemed so—so familiar, as if she really had made love with him before. 'Vikki, I'm just not sure what happened,' she choked.

'I doubt he's the sort of man who would

disclaim making love if you really had,' Vikki derided.

'He isn't the sort of man who needs another notch in his bedpost, if that's what you mean.'

A strange expression flickered in Vikki's eyes. 'You liked him,' she stated incredulously.

'No, I——' She frowned. 'I don't like him. But I'm confused by him. What happened——'

'Hasn't happened since Harry,' her friend finished gently.

The sexual torment she had known in Caleb Steele's arms was nothing like the joy she had always known in Harry's arms. But it had been so intense, and for those few brief minutes she had felt more alive than she had for a very long time. It unnerved her.

She shook off her feelings of confusion, determined to put the incident behind her. 'He's refused to introduce me to his father.' She stood up to strip off her gown and pull on fitted denims and a black jumper, releasing her hair from inside the high collar.

Vikki stood up too, realising that any more personal confidences about Caleb Steele weren't going to be forthcoming. 'Do you really need his help?' she shrugged.

'I don't know where his father is,' Cat grimaced. 'And I wouldn't feel right writing the chapter without talking to him.'

'Then you'll have to speak to Caleb Steele again.' Vikki knew better than to argue with Cat's principle of always talking to people before writing about them.

That realisation had been slowly coming to

her. She would just have to leave it long enough for Caleb to have got over last night.

The dream came to her for the first time that night.

Her arms were laden down with books, and it was all she could do to reach the doorbell, ringing it once before quickly moving her hand to stop the pile of books sliding to the floor.

She had spent most of the day at the library, had finally decided she might as well check the books out and continue working at home. Not a single bus had arrived at her stop in the twenty minutes she had waited, it was pouring down with rain, and she was very much afraid the top book was waterlogged. She just hoped it wasn't one of the really expensive ones.

Vikki opened the door just as Cat thought the books were going to tumble to the floor anyway.

'Thank goodness.' She breathed a sigh of relief as she hastily moved inside to put the books down on the telephone table in the hallway.

'My sentiments exactly!' Vikki groaned behind her. 'You're home at last!'

She turned with a frown on her face, rubbing her wet hands together to try and ward off the cold. 'What is it? The boiler didn't go again, did it?' She grimaced, the image of the hot bath she had been thinking of relaxing in, all the way home suddenly disappearing as she envisaged contacting the heating maintenance again about the boiler breaking down and leaving them with no heating and no hot water.

'It isn't the boiler,' a ruffled Vikki dismissed as

she closed the door. 'I only wish it were,' she added with feeling. 'Where have you been all this time? You said you would be back about five.'

She was well aware of the fact that it was now after seven, but Vikki didn't usually get herself in such a flap if she should happen to be late. 'You didn't get dinner ready, did you?' she sighed at the thought of the ruined meal. 'You should have said this morning, and then I——'

'I didn't get dinner ready,' Vikki interrupted impatiently. 'I just wish you had got home when you said you were going to.' She roughly helped Cat off with her wet coat.

It wasn't like her friend to get this agitated about anything. And something else occurred to Cat at the same time. 'Why are we whispering?' she whispered, having automatically lowered her voice after Vikki's initial hushed exclamation. 'Have you got a sore throat?' she asked with concern. 'You should have said——'

'I haven't got a sore throat, the boiler hasn't broken down, and dinner isn't in ruins!' Vikki was really agitated now. 'But you do have a visitor. And he's——'

'He?' she frowned warily.

'Yes, *he!*' her friend hissed. 'He's been sitting in our lounge making polite conversion for over an hour. Since I informed him you were bound to be home soon so he may as well wait! And, Cat,' she groaned her consternation. 'I actually opened the door to him in my rollers! I'd just washed my hair, and I thought it was you, and——'

'Vikki, who is my visitor?' she asked in a controlled voice, having a terrible feeling she already knew his identity. Vikki wasn't the type to get flustered for no reason, and so her visitor must be someone she didn't feel comfortable with. What was *he* doing here?

'Caleb Steele.' Her friend confirmed her thoughts. 'Oh, Cat, I've been boring him out of his mind.' She winced at the memory. 'Talking about everything and nothing. And all the time he's been replying "yes" and "no", with this cold little smile playing about his lips!'

She sighed, knowing exactly how inadequate Vikki was feeling, also knowing her friend was probably right about Caleb being bored out of his mind, remembering only too well what he had once told her about women that talked too much!

What was he doing here? she asked herself again. Two weeks had gone by since the morning he had brought her home in her evening dress. She had decided to give him another week and then contact him about another meeting. She couldn't imagine what had prompted him to come here to her.

'Did he say what he wants?' she frowned.

Vikki shrugged. 'Just to see you. He hasn't *said* much at all,' she explained shakily. 'Just sat there looking at me while I chattered on and on!' she added with mortification. 'I never thought there was such a thing as black-coloured eyes until just now!'

Those eyes were almost as unnerving as the man, Cat knew that. She squeezed Vikki's arm reassuringly. 'Don't worry, I'll take over now,' she said, with more confidence than she felt.

'I'm going out,' Vikki grabbed her coat from

the hook, hastily pulling it on. 'I told Sarah I might go round tonight; I've just decided it's an excellent idea!'

It was Caleb's fault Vikki had been driven out of her own home, the visit to her friend something she had just thought of, Cat was sure of it. Well, he could be as rude to her as he liked, but he wasn't going to treat her friends in the same way.

She picked up the pile of books and marched through to the lounge, almost faltering as her gaze clashed with a black one, her dreams suddenly a vivid reality. She had never had dreams like them before, would wake up shaking with fulfilment, knowing it was this man's lips and hands that had given her that ecstasy. They were so real, so vivid, that as she gazed at him across the room she felt as if she had known every intimacy there was with this man.

She had had those same dreams every night for the last two weeks, would deny them even to herself, only to have them return when sleep came to her. She daren't talk about them, daren't acknowledge them, had thrown herself into a frenzy of work, hoping to be too tired to dream when she finally fell asleep. It never worked.

'Cat.' Caleb stood up in one fluid movement, the green shirt tailored to him, as were the close-fitting black trousers. 'Let me take those.' He plucked the books out of her arms as if they weighed nothing at all, discarding them on to the side table. 'How have you been?'

How had she been? The last thing the two of

them had between them was politeness!

'You look terrible,' she told him with brutal honesty, lines of tiredness beside those dark eyes, deep grooves beside his grim mouth. 'Is it Luke? she asked with premonition.

He gave a ragged sigh of confirmation. 'He was involved in an accident——'

'No!' Compassion darkened her eyes.

Caleb's mouth twisted. 'Don't worry, he isn't dead,' he derided, his mouth suddenly tightening. 'Although he thought he was going to be.'

'What happened?' she prompted quietly.

'He decided to see if he could fly his car off the top of a bridge!'

She swallowed hard. 'Drugs?'

'Who knows?' his father grated. 'I didn't come here to talk about that, only to tell you that when he thought he was on his death bed he decided to confess his sins!'

'Oh.'

'Is that all?' His eyes widened. 'My son tells me he got several of his female guests to undress you and put you in my bed after you passed out from drinking vodka and orange juice and all you can say is "oh"!'

She shrugged, turning away, grateful at least that it wasn't Luke himself who had undressed her and put her in his father's bed. 'I already told you that had to be what happened,' she dismissed.

'And I didn't believe you,' Caleb snapped. 'Once Luke is walking again—he broke a leg,' he explained at her questioning look. 'Once he's back on his feet I'm going to knock him off them again! Do you realise the gravity of what he did to you that night?'

'Do you?' she returned softly.

His mouth was tight. 'When I climbed into that bed all I knew was that there was a warm and inviting woman there. You were lucky I was too tired to do anything about it!'

It didn't matter that he hadn't made love to her that night, he made love to her every other night, in her dreams! 'You really didn't have to come here——'

'Of course I did,' he scowled. 'I owe you an apology.'

And how difficult he was finding it to make it! Regret and remorse didn't sit well on his shoulders at all. 'Take it as said,' she dismissed. 'Now if you wouldn't mind I'd like to take a bath and get warm?' She was aware that her hair was drying in wild disorder.

He frowned. 'What are you doing with all these books?'

Her mouth twisted. 'Research. "Looking up the history of the time, it's all in there",' she derided.

His eyes were cold. 'Afraid of hard work, Miss Howard?'

'Not at all, Mr Steele,' she returned as formally. 'But it would be so much easier if I could just talk to your father.'

'I realise that,' he nodded. 'But as I've told you before, my father doesn't see anyone.'

'Why?' she frowned.

'He has his reasons,' Caleb dismissed harshly.

Cat sighed. 'I'm sure he does. But not being

able to talk to him is making it very difficult for me to write about him.' The preliminary work she had done on the chapter had come out very stiff and documented, rather than the interesting flow she was aiming for.

'I'm sorry.'

The lack of sincerity in his voice made her stiffen. 'You've made your apology . . .' she said pointedly.

'No, I haven't,' he derided. 'Have dinner with me?'

'Why?' she returned suspiciously.

He shrugged. 'As part of my apology for misjudging you.'

'No, thank you,' she refused primly. 'I have to take a bath, and then I have some work to do. And I'm sure you would like to go and visit your son.'

'I've just been with him.' Black eyes compelled her to look at him. 'I want to have dinner with you, little cat.'

She swallowed hard. 'Why?' she asked again.

Caleb looked exasperated with her suspicion. 'Because I haven't eaten, your friend said you haven't eaten, and it would be nice if we could eat together.'

No time spent with this man could ever be described as nice. Exciting, electric, even nerve-racking, but never *nice*! 'I usually just grab a sandwich——'

'I can see that.' His dark gaze swept over her disparagingly.

Cat looked down at herself self-consciously. She was a little on the slender side, as the

clinging black jumper and black cords clearly
showed, but it wasn't an unhealthy thin. 'I
thought I was perfect?' she reminded him
mockingly.

'You are,' he nodded abruptly. 'You're also
pale and hollow-cheeked. You could use a little
healthy food inside you.'

'Mr Steele——'

'I thought we settled that,' he drawled. 'You
can't possibly be that formal with a man you've
slept with,' he derided. 'And I do mean slept.'

She blushed. 'I don't want to go out to dinner
with you,' she told him firmly. 'Whatever your
name is!'

His lips curved into that rare smile. 'You know
what my name is, little cat,' he drawled. 'And if you
don't feel like going out we could always stay here
and eat. Although I'd want something more
substantial than a sandwich,' he added mockingly.

'You are not having any sort of dinner here.'
She spoke precisely, so that there should be no
mistake as to her meaning.

'You aren't thinking this out, Cat,' he drawled
confidently. 'Just think, you could spend the
entire evening trying to get information out of me
about my parents' marriage.'

She knew as well as he did that she wouldn't
get any information out of him that he didn't
want to tell her! 'If you would like to give me a
formal interview,' she bit out, 'I'd be happy to fit
in with your other appointments. But I'm
not having dinner with you on the off-chance
that you may make the occasional remark about
your parents that you can instantly refute as soon

as I try to print it!'

He scowled with annoyance. 'I *want* you to have dinner with me,' he rasped.

She knew that, felt as if she knew this man very well from her dreams. 'And I've refused,' she pointed out dismissively.

'Several times,' he acknowledged impatiently. 'You've been trying to see me for months, and now that I'm giving you the opportunity *you* turn *me* down!'

What she being foolish to do so? The night she had spent in his bed hadn't been his fault, and he couldn't be held responsible for the vividness of her wanton dreams about him either! And there was always the possibility that he might decide to talk about his parents.

'Can you wait while I bath and dress?' she asked awkwardly.

Triumph glittered in the dark eyes, although it was quickly masked, his mouth twisted mockingly. 'I can wait,' he murmured.

Cat gave him a sharp look, but could read nothing from his expression. And yet for a moment, a very brief moment, she had sensed something else in his words. She shook her head dismissively, sure she must have imagined it. And yet what did *he* get out of the evening if not her!

'Caleb,' she spoke slowly. 'What do *you* want?'

'Want?' he repeated cautiously.

'Yes.'

'I'm not sure I——'

'Why do you, who have avoided me for months, suddenly want to take me to dinner?' She watched him frowningly.

'I want *you*.'

She gasped, unable to hide her surprise. 'Me?' she repeated faintly, stunned at his blunt honesty.

'Yes,' he confirmed grimly. 'Even before Luke told me the truth about that night I knew I had to see you again. But first Luke had his accident, and then another union row broke out, and I couldn't seem to get away. But all that time I've been seeing you, naked, in my arms. I want you, Cat.'

'No——'

'I realise I have to evict the ghost from your bed before I can even hope to join you there myself,' he rasped. 'But I can be a patient man when I want something badly enough.'

She shook her head, wordlessly denying him and the things he was saying.

'He's dead, Cat,' Caleb told her with deliberate cruelty. 'And you're young and beautiful and alive.'

'I love him,' she choked. 'I'll always love him.'

His mouth thinned. 'He's never coming back,' he told her harshly.

She was breathing raggedly. 'That's no reason for me to let you into my life,' she said angrily. 'I don't even like you!'

'You like me to make love to you,' he taunted.

All the colour drained from her face. 'I—you—what do you mean?' He couldn't know about those dreams, no one could!

'That morning in my bed . . .' He stepped closer, the heat of his body touching her. 'If Luke hadn't walked in when he did we would have made love completely. Well?' he prompted as she made no answer.

'Yes,' she acknowledged dully. 'We would. But you only want me now because I'm a challenge, a novelty, a woman who's still in love with a dead man!'

Black eyes searched the quiet stillness of her face. 'You believe that?' he said heavily.

'Yes.'

He sighed. 'Forget dinner,' he turned on his heel. 'I've suddenly lost my appetite.'

That night Cat dreamt that Caleb came to her again.

'For goodness' sake,' Vikki chided as Cat chewed worriedly on her bottom lip. 'It's what you wanted, isn't it?'

Cat read the letter in front of her for what must have been the dozenth time since its arrival that morning. Caleb had agreed to see her for a few minutes the following afternoon. Why?

It was over a week since the night he had left her home so abruptly, and she had heard nothing from him since that time, hadn't expected to hear from him again. He wasn't a man who was usually told no!

This letter from his office, granting her an interview, had come completely out of the blue, and she couldn't help but feel suspicious about his motives. But the chapter on his parents still wasn't going well.

'Cat?' Vikki prompted.

'Yes,' she sighed, 'it's what I wanted.'

'But?'

She hadn't told her friend everything about the evening Caleb had come here, omitting the latter part of their conversation, still too unnerved by it herself.

'Why now?' she frowned.

'Why not?' Vikki shrugged. 'He's met you, realised you aren't going to exploit what you're told; I'm not at all surprised he's agreed to talk to you.'

She was; knew that when Caleb had left that night he had no intention of seeing her again. What had changed his mind? If he had, the letter only said he had agreed to see her, it didn't say what it was about.

'His photograph was in the paper today, did you see it?' Vikki prompted.

Yes, she had seen it. Luke had been leaving hospital, his leg still in plaster, his father driving the car, Luke in the back with a clinging red-head. But it had been Caleb that held her attention, grim-faced and remote. The last thing she had expected was this letter from his office.

'Luke looked well,' she dismissed.

'He looked an idiot,' Vikki scorned. 'The newspaper report said he drove over the side of a bridge,' she said disbelievingly.

'Yes,' she frowned, wondering if he had done it deliberately, because of the emotional un-happiness he was going through. She had been there too long herself not to know the despair he was feeling.

'They also implied his car wasn't the only thing that was as high as a kite.' Vikki looked at her enquiringly.

'I wouldn't know,' she dismissed. 'Do you really think I should go to this meeting?' She abruptly changed the subject, not willing to discuss Luke's emotional trauma even with Vikki.

'Of course you should go.' Her friend sounded scandalised she should even think of refusing. 'Why shouldn't you?' she frowned.

Because the dreams hadn't stopped; because she went to bed every night with feelings of trepidation and anticipation. Caleb was always there, never Harry.

'You're right,' she decided firmly. 'Why shouldn't I?'

There seemed any number of reasons why she shouldn't as she dressed the next day, but she refused to listen to any of them. She had a job to do, and it seemed Caleb was now willing to help her do it. She *wouldn't* look beyond that.

The previous evening she and Vikki had picked out the clothes she should wear, the black woollen suit feminine but formal. She decided at the last moment that she looked more efficient with her hair up, although several silky tendrils insisted on curling about her cheeks and nape.

She checked her appearance in the full-length mirror before leaving, her sparkling green eyes adorned only by the thick dark lashes, her complexion creamy, her lip-gloss a vivid plum colour. She looked elegantly slender in the woollen top and skirt, her legs long, made to look even more so in the high-heeled sandals. She looked smart enough for a business meeting. And she was determined that that was all this would be.

The Steele office suite was all that she had thought it would be, very luxurious, very efficiently run, and very much Caleb Steele's domain. He ran the English section of his businesses from here, several assistants also in residence to deal with those business holdings. The woman that identified herself as his personal secretary was beautiful enough to have been a film star herself, and Cat instantly recognised her as the woman who had politely but firmly rejected all her previous telephone requests to meet Caleb. If the other woman was aware of those rejections now she gave no sign of it, her manner one of polite friendliness.

Cat wished she possessed some of the other woman's cool confidence as she sat in the reception area waiting for the time Caleb would ring through to say she could go in.

He seemed to be taking his time about it. Was it deliberate? She didn't think he was the sort of man who would stoop to playing games like that just to unnerve a woman who had already made such a nuisance of herself. But the waiting only increased her tension, so that by the time the buzzer sounded on his secretary's desk she was nervous enough to physically jump up from her chair.

The secretary looked up to smile at her. 'Mr Steele will see you now.'

She gave a tight answering smile before moving to the wide wooden doors that were the entrance to Caleb's office. She had woken this morning with the feel of his hands on her body, the touch of his lips on her flesh, and facing him now was the last thing she wanted to do when those memories were still so vivid.

She gave a firm knock on the door before entering.

This office was like something off a film set: opulent armchairs in cream leather placed in front of the flaming log fire, a deep pile carpet that her shoes instantly sank into, a large oak desk in front of a book-lined wall. The man seated behind the desk looked at her coldly as her gaze finally turned on him.

Cat let her breath out in a ragged sigh, grateful for the fact that Caleb looked like a stranger in the dark grey business suit, his expression hard and forbidding, his eyes icy, and nothing like the Caleb of her dreams who seduced her with his body.

'I'm sorry if you were kept waiting.' He spoke dismissively. 'I was on the telephone when you arrived.'

'I didn't mind.' Her own voice was husky from the intimate thoughts she had just had.

'Please, sit down.' He indicated the straight-backed chair facing him across his desk.

She did so, her thoughts racing. How could they act like strangers when they were far from that!

'Are you still having the dreams?'

Her panicked gaze flew to his face, all colour draining from her cheeks. 'Dreams?' she repeated in a strangulated voice.

'About Harry's accident,' he nodded. 'You look like a decent night's sleep wouldn't do you any harm.'

'You don't look too good yourself,' she was stung into replying, deeply relieved that he hadn't been talking about her dreams of *him*. He couldn't know that not even the nightmares of Harry came to her any more.

'I'd lay odds on my sleepless nights being due to an entirely different reason to yours,' he derided hardly.

And he would be wrong! 'I didn't come here to talk about the way I look, Mr Steele,' she snapped. 'You seemed to think we had something to discuss?'

'Yes.' His mouth compressed, the black eyes glittering. 'I have some good news for you. And some bad news,' he added drily.

'This sounds like a very bad joke,' she scorned.

'Not mine, I assure you,' Caleb rasped. 'Luke has been up to mischief again.'

Cat felt herself stiffen warily, remembering all too vividly where that young man's 'mischief' had left her last time. 'Yes?' she prompted with obvious reluctance.

Caleb sighed. 'He told his grandfather about your requests to meet him.'

'Oh?'

'Which brings us to the good news,' he dismissed mockingly.

Her eyes widened eagerly. 'He's agreed to see me?' she gasped.

'Yes,' Caleb ground out, as if he weren't at all pleased at the idea.

Her pleasure at that glowed in her eyes, only to be dulled again as she realised she hadn't yet heard the 'bad news'. It meant there had to be some sort of condition attached to the meeting.

'He's agreeable to talking about his marriage to your mother?' she prompted for this much at least.

'Subject to reading and approving what you write, yes,' Caleb rasped.

'What else?' she frowned, sure that wasn't the 'bad news'; she had already assured Caleb she would do that anyway. She had no intention of upsetting or hurting anyone.

He leaned back in his chair, watching her with narrowed eyes. 'You know that my father has chosen to shut himself away from the world in recent years?'

'Of course,' she nodded slowly, wary of what was to come.

'Well, he isn't in London.'

'I see.'

'Do you?' Caleb scorned. 'I very much doubt that you do.'

'Then why don't you get on with it and tell me instead of playing this guessing game with me!' she snapped in her tension, colour entering her cheeks as she realised what she had done. 'I'm sorry,' she said abruptly. 'I—it's just that this means a lot to me,' she excused lamely.

His mouth was tight, his eyes cold. 'My father has asked me to issue you with an invitation for you to stay with him this weekend.'

'Why, that's wonder——'

'Cat,' he flatly cut in on her enthusiasm. 'All you will know about your destination is that you won't leave Britain!'

CHAPTER FOUR

CAT frowned. 'And just what does that mean?'

'Isn't it obvious?' he returned snappingly. 'If you want to meet my father you will get yourself to the airport at six-thirty tomorrow evening.'

Airport? 'I thought you said he was in Britain?'

'He is,' Caleb sighed. 'But Britain is a big place, and a flight will be quicker and less tiring. And don't try and work out where he could be if you have to fly there,' he derided, as she could be seen doing just that. 'We could just fly you around in circles for a couple of hours and land nearby.'

She pulled a face. 'Isn't all this a little dramatic?'

He shrugged broad shoulders. 'How long is it since my father spoke to a reporter?'

Ten years. Lucien Steele had hidden himself away completely for the last two years of that time, but he had refused to be interviewed a long time before that. His books, huge blockbusters about Hollywood and the people that existed in that glittery world, were always bestsellers, the fact that the author had lived in that world and now refused to talk about it making them avid reading. But rumours of ghost-writers had abounded the last few years simply because he locked himself away and wouldn't see anyone.

Cat knew she was very privileged to be allowed to meet him. If only the meeting weren't made to seem so mysterious.

'I need hardly add,' Caleb rasped, 'that I'm completely against the idea.'

That had been obvious from the first. Whatever attraction he had professed to feel for her last week was now superseded by his harsh disapproval of this proposed visit to his father. And for that she was extremely grateful. Maybe now the dreams would stop.

'I'll go,' she decided firmly.

Black eyes narrowed. 'Just like that?' he bit out. 'You'll fly off to God knows where for the weekend and yet you refused to even have dinner with me!'

Her mouth twisted. 'I think a weekend with your father would be less dangerous than dinner with you,' she taunted.

That rare warmth darkened his eyes, the anger going from his face as he began to smile. 'You're probably right,' he drawled. 'I haven't changed my mind about you, little cat,' he added softly.

So much for that supposition! 'Neither have I,' Her eyes flashed.

He gave an appreciative inclination of his head for her show of temper. 'Bringing you round to wanting what I want could prove an interesting battle.'

'One you would be predestined to lose,' she assured him confidently.

'Ah yes,' he pursed his lips. 'Any man would find it difficult to fight the ghost of a previous lover!'

Cat stiffened at the derision in his tone. 'Harry was my life,' she bit out.

'And would he have wanted you to waste what was left of it?'

She breathed raggedly. 'I told you, I enjoy my life as it is.'

Caleb stood up, and she involuntarily took a step backwards, her nervousness increasing at the predatory look that entered his eyes at her movement. He came round the desk now to stand in front of her, his hands reaching for her.

'No——'

'I don't like women flinching away from me, little cat,' he murmured throatily. 'Especially when I can so easily stroke you and make you purr.'

Panic widened her eyes, and she took another step backwards, only to feel her calf press up against something soft before she felt herself overbalance and fall down into one of the leather armchairs.

Caleb stook over her looking down, blocking her exit. 'Do you know how long it is since I allowed thoughts of a woman, any woman, to disturb my nights?' he rasped. 'Since I reached out for a certain woman's body only to find she wasn't there?'

Cat swallowed hard, apprehension in her eyes. If he should touch her——

'Years, little cat,' he murmured self-derisively. 'I'm sorry the man you loved died, Cat,' he added huskily, 'but I'm very much alive, and wanting you is killing me!'

She gasped as he came down in the chair

beside her, the length of his body pressed against her.

'Cat.' He gently cupped her chin and turned her to face him, his expression gentle. 'I didn't plan for this to happen,' he groaned. 'I thought I could see you again, put my father's proposition to you, and then forget about you. But I can't, Cat. I can't!'

Cat watched in fascination as his head bent towards hers, seeing that his eyes weren't really black after all but a deep, deep blue. And they were coming closer and closer and closer . . .

His lips parted hers, and as they did so Cat realised this was the first time his mouth had touched hers; that first morning he had caressed only her breasts. His mouth on hers wasn't at all as she had imagined it would be; it was warm and inviting, moving with infinite gentleness against hers. Her eyes closed, and it was just like her dreams; the scent of him, the feel of him, his shoulders firm beneath her hands as she clung to him.

His mouth moved moistly across her cheek and down her throat, his hair smelling of lemons as it brushed against her, his teeth nibbling the sensitive hollows of her throat, the caressing motion of his hand faltering beneath the curve of her breast, his thumb stroking against the hardening nub.

She cradled him into her as she felt the warmth from the fire touch her bared skin, only to know a burning sensation through to her thighs as one taut nipple was suckled into his eager mouth, his tongue caressing her in circular movements.

Her breathing was ragged as she arched against him, needing more, wanting more, *receiving* more as his hand cupped her other breast. She was lost, on fire, reality and dreams becoming one, and she couldn't stop either one of them.

A loud cracking noise wrenched Caleb's head up in a startled movement, his eyes black with passion, his lips moist with the taste of her.

'Damn,' he muttered impatiently, bending down to pick up the hot splinter of wood that had been thrown from the fire, tossing it back amongst the flames before turning back to Cat.

'I—I thought it was an artificial one,' she croaked inadequately.

'No,' he replied with surprising intensity. 'It's very real.'

Bewildered green eyes gazed up into black ones, and she quickly turned away from whatever he was trying to say to her in those expressive depths, grateful to him as she felt the softness of her jumper pulled down over her aching breasts, tears flooding her eyes as he stood up.

'I dislike anything false, Cat,' he spoke raspingly. 'And you're so very real.'

She straightened in the chair, not able to face him yet, not able to face *herself* yet! 'Except the dyed eyelashes,' she reminded him sharply.

His mouth twisted. 'Everyone is allowed at least one artifice,' he drawled. 'Everything else about you is very real.'

Including her response to him! No matter how she tried to deny it she couldn't refuse this man anything he asked of her.

'Including my love for Harry,' she said in a

hard voice, hoping he would forgive her for using him as a shield in this shameless way.

Caleb's mouth tightened. 'You can only beat me with that stick so many times, Cat, before it ceases to have any effect,' he warned gratingly.

Her chin went up in challenge. 'Did it work this time?'

'Yes!'

'Then I have no reason to suppose it will be put to the test again,' she told him coldly. 'I doubt the two of us will meet again.'

He smiled without humour. 'You think I'm going to back off?'

'I don't think you have too much choice about it,' she scorned.

'No?' he queried softly.

She felt a flutter of apprehension in her stomach. She had known she shouldn't come here today. Next time she would listen to her own reasoning! 'I have to leave now.' She stood up, self-consciously straightening her clothing. 'Will someone meet me at the airport tomorrow evening?' she asked, with much more calm than she felt.

Caleb frowned. 'You'll still go?'

'Of course,' she nodded distantly.

'Good,' he said admiringly. 'I wondered if my persistence might have put you off.'

'This—has nothing to do with my meeting your father,' she bit out tautly.

'I couldn't agree more.' He moved to sit back behind his desk. 'Yes, someone will meet you at the airport. And pack warm clothing,' he advised. 'The forecast is snow. Everywhere,' he taunted, as she tried to remember where they had forecast snow on the radio this morning.

He was right, it had been everywhere; this was one of the worst Februarys England had had in years. 'Will the plane be able to take off in such extreme weather?' she frowned.

Caleb shrugged. 'The snow forecast was for the weekend.'

'But——'

'I'll let you know if the plans change,' he derided. 'After all, I know where you live.'

Why did everything this man said sound like a threat? 'Very well,' she accepted coolly. 'I—er—thank you,' she added awkwardly, because she didn't know what else to say.

Amusement glittered in his eyes. 'You're very welcome,' he drawled.

'I meant for arranging for me to see your father,' she snapped irritably.

He raised innocent brows. 'Of course.'

Damn the man. What did he think she meant!

'It isn't funny,' she chided Vikki indignantly as her friend couldn't seem to stop laughing.

'Of course it is,' Vikki chuckled. 'He actually made love to you there, in his office? And you said thank you!'

Her cheeks blushed fiery red. 'I wish I'd never told you about it now,' she said irritably. But she had had to talk to someone about what had happened, and Vikki was her closest friend.

'I'm not laughing at you, Cat,' her friend soothed. 'I just can't imagine the man I met acting that way. He seemed so—controlled,' she explained.

'He is,' she sighed. 'He's just decided I'm to be his next victim.'

'He doesn't sound like a rapist or a murderer to me,' Vikki laughed.

'You know what I meant,' she said impatiently.

'Yes,' her friend still smiled. 'And if you're so anxious to avoid seeing him again why are you going ahead with this meeting with his father?'

'Because Caleb isn't going to be there!'

'Did he say he wasn't?'

'No. But——'

'You should try reading the gossip columns for a change, Cat,' Vikki teased. 'Apparently he *flies* himself all over the world. You did say you were flying to this meeting, didn't you?' She raised questioning eyebrows.

'But he wouldn't——' she broke off, frowning. Caleb hadn't said he would be present during her meeting with his father, but then again he hadn't said he wouldn't be either! She sighed her frustration. 'I'm going to telephone him right now and ask,' she decided determinedly.

Vikki frowned. 'Do you really think he would tell you if he wants you that badly?'

Remembering his aversion to any form of artifice she nodded, sure Caleb wouldn't lie even if it might mean she changed her mind about the weekend.

Caleb was no longer in his office, and his secretary wasn't expecting him back until late next week.

Cat was satisfied with that, safe in the knowledge that Caleb was back in America.

Although, in some ways, she wished he were at

her side the next evening when she arrived at the airport. She had no idea who was meeting her, where they were going, or how Lucien Steele would receive her when they did arrive.

'Miss Howard,' greeted a familiar voice.

She turned, colour heightening her cheeks as she looked at the man she knew only as Norm, remembering that on the last occasion she had met him she had been at a distinct disadvantage. Obviously he remembered it too!'

Sympathy for her predicament gleamed in his eyes. 'I'm sure that, whatever did happen that night, Caleb met his match,' he said, taking her luggage easily into his hand.

'Yes.' A smile curved her lips as she relaxed a little.

'Is this all you have with you?' He indicated the single small suitcase of hers that he held.

'What more could I need for a weekend— wherever?' she dismissed.

'True.' He grinned at her effort at appearing nonchalant in the face of flying off into the blue with a complete stranger.

'Norm——'

His smile faded. 'I have instructions not to, Cat,' he interrupted regretfully.

She nodded. 'And you always do what Caleb tells you to do.'

Amusement gleamed in his eyes once again. 'Within reason,' he drawled.

She liked this man, Cat decided. He must feel as awkward about this situation as she did, and yet he could still maintain his sense of humour.

'I'm sorry,' she smiled. 'That was unfair of me.'

'A little.' Blue eyes twinkled. 'But it was worth a try, hm?'

'Yes,' she laughed. 'I'm glad you're the one to meet me; I was feeling a little nervous.'

'I would never have guessed that,' he teased.

She ruefully acknowledged the truth of his mockery, knew her eyes were too deep a green, her movements too jerky, her usual good humour replaced by sharp suspicion. It just served to confirm what she had always known: she would have made a lousy investigative reporter! But the mystery surrounding this meeting with Lucien Steele certainly had her adrenalin pumping—and her nerves jumping. Which Norm had lightly acknowledged with his mockery.

'Maybe we should introduce ourselves properly?' he suggested gently. 'Our last meeting wasn't exactly conducive to polite introductions,' he recognised ruefully. 'I'm Norman Bruce, Norm to my friends, which I hope you will be. I'm also Caleb's personal assistant.'

'And I'm Catherine Howard—Caleb's thorn in his side!'

He chuckled softly. 'I had noticed he's been going around like a wounded lion the last few weeks.'

Colour darkened her cheeks as she remembered that Caleb had said she had been constantly on his mind since that morning in his bedroom. 'I don't have the figure to be Daniel!' she returned sharply.

'I don't think you're that sort of thorn,' Norm mocked.

She doubted that Caleb was the sort of man to discuss personal problems with anyone, but it was obvious he had been in enough of an uncharacteristic mood for Norman Bruce to have realised something was bothering him, that the other man had also been astute enough to realise *she* was the problem. Caleb really was serious about wanting her!

'Hey, this is really none of my business,' Norm encouraged, seeing her frowning countenance.

Cat followed him across the tarmac to the waiting plane. 'I just don't want you to think I'm——'

'I know exactly what you are, Cat,' he cut in firmly. 'You're the writer that wants to meet Lucien—if you were anything else Caleb wouldn't be growling so loudly,' he teased.

Cat had almost stumbled up the plane's steps before she realised what she was doing. This sleek silver machine wasn't the commercial jet running a domestic flight that she had been expecting, and the Steele Film Studio logo was vividly emblazoned on the tail.

She clutched at Norm's arm. 'Caleb's plane?' It was difficult to make herself heard in this noisy part of the airport, planes constantly coming and going, the silver jet ready for take-off, just waiting for its passenger—her!

'Of course.' Norm seemed surprised that she should need to question that.

She made no effort to climb up the stairway to the interior. 'Who's flying it?'

A frown darkened his brow. 'The pilot,' he derided drily.

Cat looked up at the cockpit, but she couldn't make out any faces, only movement. 'Caleb——'

'Is not flying the plane,' Norm assured her mockingly.

'He isn't on board?' Somehow she trusted this man to tell her the truth.

'He isn't even in the country,' he drawled.

She smiled her relief, hurriedly preceding him on to the plane, glad she had dressed warmly now; the wind was icy.

The interior of the plane had obviously been fitted out to Caleb's personal needs, the eight luxurious seats arranged in such a way that they were positioned about two tables, probably so that people could work during the flight. Another larger area had been made into a small lounge. They were certainly going to travel in comfort!

Cat had never flown before, the honeymoon she and Harry had intended taking in Greece the closest she had ever come to an air trip. She had felt no interest in travel since that time. She found that she liked it, could feel the excitement building within her, meeting Norm's indulgent look with gleaming eyes.

'Your first flight,' he guessed wryly.

'But not my last,' she assured him enthusiastically. 'This is wonderful!' She had had a wonderful view of the capital's lights as they took off, and they were even now cruising above the clouds as she and Norm sipped the drinks the attendant had brought them, the sky blue-black up here. Strangely, it reminded Cat of Caleb's eyes.

'Short flights are fine,' Norm nodded. 'It's the ones to the States that are killers.'

Her expression became dreamy. 'I'd love to see America!'

'Who knows?' He watched her closely. 'Maybe you will one day.'

'No, I—no,' she said again more forcefully as she realized what he meant. 'I have no wish to go anywhere with your employer!'

He stood up to stretch his long legs. 'I get the impression there are a lot of things he would like to show you,' he mocked.

Cat turned away, staring fixedly out of the window, looking straight at the sky that reminded her of blue-black eyes.

He hadn't come to her last night.

She had lain in bed re-living those moments in his office, fighting the sleep that wanted to claim her, not wanting his arms about her again, his kisses as he brought her to fulfilment. But she hadn't been able to push back the realms of sleep.

And nothing had happened.

She had begun to search for him in the dark corners of her mind, could even now recall her nightgown-clad body running frantically about in the darkness, a pale ethereal figure with despair etched into her face. She had woken sobbing.

And Caleb hadn't come to her.

What was he doing to her! For nights she had wished him gone from her dreams, had felt ashamed of her wanton thoughts about him. And this morning she had cried because he had gone!

'Cat? Are you all right?' Norm's concerned voice cut in on her tortuous thoughts.

She opened her eyes, blinking, realising as she did so that her lashes were damp with fresh tears. 'I'm fine,' she dismissed abruptly. 'Are we nearly there?'

'About another twenty minutes,' he replied vaguely, frowning at her. 'Are you feeling airsick?'

If only it were as simple as that! She didn't know *what* was wrong with her, had been in one state of turmoil or another since the moment she had met Caleb Steele. And it wasn't getting any better!

'Not at all,' she dismissed briskly. 'Will Mr Steele have any other guests this weekend?' she asked interestedly.

'Mr Steele never has guests,' Norm informed her bluntly. 'I have a feeling that the only reason he agreed to see you was because of what Luke told him.'

She frowned. 'I know that he told his grandfather I wanted to meet him, but I can't see anything odd in that,' she said warily.

He shrugged. 'I'm not speaking out of line when I say Luke has a penchant for making mischief . . .'

'No,' she acknowledged, already very familiar with that side of that young man.

'And you can bet on it that, whatever did happen the night of his birthday party, he's embellished it enough to make his grandfather interested in meeting the lady involved.'

'Oh no!' All the colour drained from her cheeks, humiliation washing over her at the thought of the famous author knowing of the embarrassing events of that night. 'If I were a man I'd punch Luke Steele on the mouth,' she snapped with feeling.

'If you were a man the situation wouldn't have arisen,' Norm derided.

If she had been a man in his bed that night Caleb Steele would have done the punching—and it wouldn't have been his son at the receiving end of it!

But he must have been aware of what Luke had told his grandfather. How could he have put her in this embarrassing position! Quite easily, a little voice mocked, he had some debts of his own to repay.

'I thought Lucien Steele just wanted to meet me because he approved of what I want to write.' She groaned at her naïveté.

'Maybe he does,' Norm shrugged. 'But fore-warned is forearmed, as the saying goes.'

She wanted to tell him to instruct the pilot to turn the plane around and take her back home, but she was damned if she would give Luke *or* Caleb Steele that satisfaction.

'What does it matter why he's agreed to see me?' she grated. 'As long as he does.'

Admiration gleamed in pale blue eyes, and Norm smiled his approval, glancing up as a light flashed on at the front of the plane. 'Fasten your seatbelt, Cat, we'll be landing very shortly.'

That sounded very final, giving her no choice. She would meet Lucien Steele no matter what Luke had told him! And she would get her interview. Damn Caleb for doing this to her!

'Landings aren't much worse than taking off,'

Norm squeezed her hand reassuringly, mistaking the reason for her tension.

No sooner had the plane touched down than the door was opened, she was ushered down the steps by a now brisk Norman Bruce, the chauffeur opening the door for her to climb into the back of the waiting limousine while Norm supervised their luggage being put into the boot.

They weren't running any risk of her finding out which airport this was. She actually wouldn't put it past Caleb to have done what he said and had her flown around in circles!

But it soon became obvious that they were nowhere near London, hardly any time passing at all before they were out of the built-up area and out into open road, the skyline hilly and becoming mountainous. She turned excitedly to Norm, silenced by the rueful rise of his brows. He was right, it wasn't fair to press him for their whereabouts.

The inside of the car was lovely and warm, which was more than could be said for outside. Heavy snow already lay on the ground, and it was just starting to fall again softly. Scotland or Wales was Cat's guess. She didn't really care which anyway; had no interest in exposing Lucien Steele's hideaway even if she should discover where it was.

They were driving up a tree-lined driveway now, heavy snow reflected in the headlights, Cat gasping as she saw what lay at the end of that driveway. It looked like a medieval castle!

She stood and gazed at it in silent awe while Norm and the chauffeur organised the luggage.

Thick, greystone walls, feet thick, she would guess, lights burning in several of the small diamond-shaped windows, illuminating the beauty of the long sprawling building. It was magnificent!

'Welcome to my home, Cat,' a softly familiar voice greeted.

She wrenched her gaze around in the direction of that voice. Caleb!

CHAPTER FIVE

SHE barely gave herself time to register how darkly satanic he looked as he stood in the doorway, dressed in a thick black jumper and black trousers, before turning her accusing gaze on Norm.

He sighed as he knew the reason for that accusation. 'He isn't a guest, Cat; this is Caleb's house.'

And he hadn't lied when he said Caleb was out of the country either; both Wales and Scotland counted as countries in their own right as far as the inhabitants were concerned.

'Come inside out of the snow, Cat,' Caleb prompted. 'You can berate Norm later for any erroneous impressons he may have given you.' He gave the other man an amused look.

Cat didn't move. 'I think I would like to be taken back to London,' she bit out tautly.

The amusement instantly faded from black eyes. 'Why?'

'It's obvious you had me brought here under false pretences, and I——'

'Excuse us, Norm, Hector,' Caleb grated at the same time as he moved to grasp Cat's arm, pulling her inside the house, across the wide reception area and into a warmly comfortable lounge, the log fire burning in the huge grate mainly responsible for that. The room was big and airy, scatter rugs on the wooden floor, the old and comfortable furniture fitting in exactly with the starkness of stone-grey walls and the huge wooden chandelier hanging from the high ceiling.

'Let—me—go.' Cat pulled out of his grasp. 'You——'

'I don't need to trick a woman into spending the weekend with me, Catherine Howard,' Caleb told her forcefully. 'They're all too damned willing!'

She blinked in the face of his vicious anger. 'You—you mean your father really is here?'

'Yes,' he rasped.

'But——'

'It's my house but my father has made it his home,' he cut in coldly. 'You haven't been brought here to amuse me for the weekend!'

Colour darkened her cheeks. 'There's no need to mock——'

'If I don't I'm likely to take your pretty neck between my hands and squeeze the life out of you instead!' Black eyes glittered coldly.

She could see that she really had infuriated him, frowning her confusion. 'You did make sure that both your office and Norm gave me the impression you had gone to America,' she accused. 'And you deliberately omitted to tell me you intended being here.' She looked at him challengingly.

'I'm here at my father's request,' he snapped. 'He's out of the practice of entertaining guests, especially young ladies.'

Her mouth tightened. 'You do realise that he thinks we're—that we're——'

'Lovers,' he gave a mocking inclination of his head. 'Five minutes in your company and he'll know that isn't true!' he derided.

She bristled indignantly at his dismissive tone. 'What do you mean?'

Caleb's mouth twisted. 'Lovers don't act the way we do,' he rasped.

She swallowed hard. 'And how—how do we act?' she frowned.

'*I* act as if I want you.' His eyes were narrowed. 'And *you* act as if you hate that want. My father is an astute man, he'll soon realise Luke was lying in his insinuations.'

But would he? If Lucien Steele were that astute would he see the memory of her dreams in her eyes? No, of course he wouldn't; people couldn't see dreams in your eyes!

She shook her head. 'I can't stay here now.'

'Why the hell not?' he demanded impatiently.

She flinched at his anger. 'This whole thing was ridiculous from the first——'

'And yet you agreed to it,' he reminded curtly.

'I thought I would spend a pleasant weekend talking to your father, get my information, and go home.' She sighed at her naïveté. She should have known Caleb would do something like this.

'You can still do that,' he bit out.

'No,' she shook her head. 'I want to return to London.'

'Not tonight,' he told her with finality.

'Why not?' she asked suspiciously.

'Because it's nine-thirty at night,' he answered with barely restrained impatience.

'I don't——'

'And my plane flew straight back to London,' he finished bluntly.

Her eyes widened. 'Oh.'

Caleb sighed. 'You were right that night when you said you're something of a novelty, Cat,' he drawled. 'No other woman I know has wanted to escape my company as desperately as you do.'

Desperation seemed to imply fear. Did he realise how nervous it made her just to be in the same room as him? A whole weekend in his company was unthinkable!

'I'm not desperate, Mr Steele,' she dismissed coldly. 'I just don't like being taken for a fool!'

He looked as if he were about to say, 'Then don't act like one!', and then thought better of it. 'I've waited dinner for you——'

'Oh, I'm not dressed to meet your father.' She looked down at the fitted denims and the sheepskin coat she still wore over her dark green jumper.

'My father ate his meal in his room over an hour ago,' he revealed drily. 'So it's only me you have to impress,' he added.

Her eyes flashed. 'Perhaps I could just go up to my room and freshen up . . .?'

'Of course.' His eyes mocked her. 'I'll take you upstairs——'

'Oh, but——'

'Relax, little cat,' he mocked. 'I make it a rule never to seduce young innocents before I've eaten,' he drawled. 'I have to put my appetites in order of priority.'

Cat hated being the object of his scorn, following him up the wide stone stairway to the second floor, and along a narrow corridor to a room at the far end of it.

'How many rooms does this house have?' She peered curiously through the door he had just opened into the room, gasping as she saw the four-poster bed that dominated the room, with its brocade curtains the same as the ones at the long windows, the heavy furniture matching the bed. 'Is this real?' She stroked the polished wood of one of the four posts with an awed hand.

'Or something manufactured for an uncouth American with more money than taste?' he drawled. 'It's real,' he bit out tersely. 'As is the rest of the furniture in the house; it was all bought at auction. As for how many rooms there are,' he shrugged. 'Who knows?' He turned to leave.

'Caleb.' She reached out a hand and touched his arm. 'I wasn't implying you had had the bed made, I—I've just never seen an original.'

His eyes darkened as he looked at her, his expression softening. 'Neither had I,' he murmured.

Cat once again had the impression he was saying more than the words implied. And then she dismissed the idea as being fanciful. It had been a very strange evening.

'Cat——'

'I think I can find my own way back to the lounge,' she assured him dismissively, her hand dropping back to her side. 'If you could give me five minutes?'

He nodded distantly, whatever he had been about to say held in check.

Five minutes or five hours, she trembled once Caleb had returned downstairs, wouldn't dispel the tingling sensation she had felt in her hand just from touching his arm! She was going mad! Where were her memories of Harry tonight, the warm glow she felt whenever she thought of him? He couldn't desert her now!

But she knew that he had. She loved him, knew that she always would, but Caleb wasn't only forcing her to feel again, he was forcing her to *live* again. And she was afraid, so very afraid.

She was also using up her five minutes—fast! She quickly brushed her hair, the snow having dampened its wildness slightly, deciding the denims and jumper would be fine to wear to dinner tonight. After all, she had only just arrived, and Caleb wasn't dressed in the least formally.

She had, as she had said, a good sense of direction, but even so she knew it would be easy to get lost in the house, it was so big. But there had been no garishly modern changes to the house that she could see; even the central heating was unobtrusive, the water boiling hot a second ago when she had rinsed her face. The house was filled with atmosphere; she could almost imagine entering the lounge to find long tables laid out with food, dogs on the floor to snap up the scraps and bones that were carelessly discarded, lusty men downing wine as they fondled the women on their knee, with a jaundiced Caleb sitting at the head of those tables as he dispassionately tried to decide which of those women he would have in his bed that night. He would fit in very well with those wild, unprincipled times.

'I'd love to know what's brought the flush to your cheeks and that sparkle to your eyes!'

She stiffened, the spell broken as she stared down at Caleb as he stood at the bottom of the stairs, his clothes of black sweater and trousers showing her it was indeed modern times, although his expression matched the cynicism of that other Caleb. She continued her descent of the stairs. 'You have a beautiful home,' she told him with a politeness that revealed none of her previous turmoil.

He straightened as she reached his side. 'And that put the flush in your cheeks and the sparkle in your eyes?' he derided.

Her mouth firmed. 'I always look this way when I'm hungry,' she snapped.

'For what?' he murmured throatily, his hand on her arm as he led the way to the dining room.

Cat came to an abrupt halt as she turned to look at him. 'If this is your idea of entertainment, Caleb, then I'd rather you didn't bother!'

He gave one of those rare grins. 'You do absolutely nothing for my ego!'

She turned away to continue walking in the direction of the double doors that seemed to lead to the dining room.

'Nothing to say?' he taunted softly.

'Nothing repeatable,' she bit out.

'You *are* hungry, aren't you?' he mused.

She glared at him, looking for the double meaning, the deliberate innocence in his widened eyes telling her there had been one. 'Caleb——'

'Let's not keep Mrs McDonald waiting any longer,' he drawled as he pushed open the doors and preceded her into what was a much smaller room than the one she had been expecting, the oval table laid with two places that faced each other across its width, the fire and the five-candled candelabra at one end of the table the only illumination in the room. Caleb glanced ruefully at Cat's face. 'I think Mrs McDonald must have got the wrong impression when I told her there would be a young lady for dinner,' he said drily, reaching for the main light switch that would turn on the wooden chandelier above the table.

'No!' Cat stopped him more harshly than she had meant to, colour darkening her cheeks as she turned away from his speculative gaze. 'I—it's nicer this way,' she mumbled awkwardly.

'I think so.' He gave an inclination of his head, moving to pull out her chair for her to sit down before pressing the button next to the fireplace in signal for their meal to be brought through.

She frowned at him across the table as he sat down. 'Norm——'

'Is in his room,' he answered with satisfaction.

'Why?' she frowned suspiciously.

Caleb sighed. 'Not through anything I've said or done I can assure you,' he rasped. 'He only got in from the States a few hours ago, and——'

'Today?' she gasped, remembering what the other man had said about how tiring he found those flights to be.

'Yes—today,' Caleb drawled.

'He must be exhausted!'

'He is,' Caleb nodded. 'And before you start berating me for working him too hard let me explain that the trip home was a personal one. It was his twentieth wedding anniversary——'

'He's married?' she gasped.

Caleb looked at her with narrowed eyes. 'Did he say or do anything on the way here that gave you the impression he wasn't a married man?'

The colour left her cheeks to come back in a blush as she realised what he was asking. 'Just because you have the morals——' She broke off abruptly as he held up a silencing hand. A small, well-rounded woman bustled into the room, smiling warmly at Cat as she placed two steaming bowls on the table in front of them. Cat smiled back at her, liking the other woman immediately. 'It isn't true what they say about the "dour Scots",' she murmured, once the other woman had returned to her kitchen.

Caleb laughed, a full-bodied laugh of enjoyment, his eyes warm, an enticing dimple appearing in his left cheek. 'What gave it away?' he mused. 'The mountains, Hector, Mrs McDonald, or the broth?'

She looked down at the creamy-grey soup in her bowl. 'Is this broth?' Her eyes glowed.

'Try it,' he encouraged.

She was careful not to burn her mouth, finding the meat soup didn't have as much taste as the manufactured varieties of soups but liking it anyway. It was hot and filling, and she really was very hungry. 'It's good,' she nodded after several mouthfuls.

'You didn't answer my question about Norm?' he prompted hardly.

Her eyes flashed. 'He was very friendly and

nice,' she defended. 'He's obviously another man that takes his marriage vows seriously.' She reminded him of the accusation he had made at their first meeting about one of his directors.

'Don't pin the break-up of my marriage on me, Cat,' he rasped. 'Deanna decided she didn't like being a wife or mother and walked out on Luke and me.'

'I'm sorry,' she grimaced. 'Everything always seems to become so personal between us.'

'Eat your broth,' he instructed gruffly.

She was relieved to do so; everything *did* become too personal between them.

She took a deep breath. 'I've decided I might as well stay on and meet your father,' she spoke at last, the companionable silence as they ate giving a false air of intimacy, her nerves getting tauter by the minute.

His mouth twisted. 'What changed your mind?'

She shrugged. 'I'm here now; it would be silly to return to London without meeting him.'

'I think so,' he nodded.

She gave him an impatient glare. 'When will I be able to see him?'

'Breakfast tomorrow,' he revealed abruptly, refusing the dessert Mrs McDonald offered, Cat accepting a large chunk of the apple pie so that the poor woman shouldn't be upset. 'But he works during the morning,' Caleb added once the cook had gone. 'So you won't get to talk to him until tomorrow afternoon at the earliest.'

She frowned. 'It seems to me that I could have arrived tomorrow.'

'Then who would I have shared this meal with?' he derided.

'Caleb——'

'Can you ski?' he smoothly interrupted as she seemed set to reprimand him once again.

Her eyes widened. 'I've never tried,' she told him truthfully.

'You will tomorrow,' he told her.

'Where?'

'The Cairngorms.'

'Are we near Aviemore?' she asked excitedly.

Caleb shrugged. 'I can't see any point in lying to you about it now. I knew once you got up here it would no longer be a secret.' He frowned. 'But I wanted you here anyway.'

Cat reached across the table and placed her hand on the back of his, finding his flesh warm and firm to the touch. 'I'm really not going to tell anyone where your father is,' she promised intently.

Black eyes stared into green, seeming to reach into her very soul and see the truth of her words. His hand turned over and he clasped her fingers in his own. 'Shall we go into the other room?' he suggested huskily.

She couldn't look away, didn't even try as they walked through to the lounge, the overhead lighting firmly switched off before they both sat down on the sofa in front of the fire.

They just sat there in companionable silence for some time, Caleb still holding her hand as they both stared at the pattern of the flames.

'Cat.'

She turned obediently at the quiet comment

in his voice, lost in the dark sensuality of his gaze.

'I know you're frightened,' he smoothed the hair back from her cheek, 'and I want you to know that however far this goes,' he gently kissed one creamy cheek, 'I won't take you.' He kissed her other cheek before claiming her mouth, groaning low in his throat as her lips parted for him.

It had been inevitable, she had known that from the moment she had allowed their meal to remain a romantic one. But she could no longer fight her need for this man's kisses, his hands on her body.

'I fantasise about kissing you here.' Caleb deftly removed her jumper, gently easing down the straps on the silky white camisole she wore instead of a bra, her breasts bare and inviting. 'I love doing this.' He took one tip into his mouth, pulling on it in painful ecstasy. 'Don't stop me yet, little cat,' he groaned, before moving to the other breast.

She stared down at his head against her creamy skin, his eyes closed in his enjoyment, dark lashes fanned out across his hard cheeks, not needing any reflection to watch him as he loved her, feeling a wealth of emotion for this man as he suckled like a child.

Her own feelings were far from maternal as he increased the pressure of his mouth, her lips parted moistly for him when he raised his head to claim them.

He followed her down on the length of the sofa as she moved on to her back, unbuttoning his shirt to pull the material aside, his hair-roughened chest arousing new sensations as her breasts nestled in the dark hair there.

'Dear God!' Caleb wrenched his mouth from hers. 'Kiss me, Cat. Love *me*!'

Her lips were tentative against the hardness of his chest, feeling the hard brown nub beneath her tongue, aware of the shudder that ran through his body as she kissed him in the way he had just kissed her. She knew her power over this man at that moment, even as she acknowledged his power over her, caressing each other now as their mouths met, the warm rasp of his tongue moving silkily into her mouth.

It was just as if he had possessed her, the thrusts of his marauding tongue matched by the rhythm of his thighs moving against hers. He was keeping his promise not to make love to her, but she could feel the heated ache in her body building to a point of release, knew that if she didn't stop this now she was going to reach fulfilment just from the caress of his mouth and body. She bit down very gently on his tongue.

'What——? No, Cat!' he groaned at the regret he read in her eyes. 'No, no, *no*!' He buried his face in the side of her throat, rigid with desire as he fought for control. 'Yes.' He finally shuddered acceptance of the end to their lovemaking. 'Yes,' he sighed again, lying heavily against her.

Cat lay beneath him not saying a word, too shaken herself to do more than just lie there.

Finally he raised his head to look at her with eyes still dark with passion. 'I very nearly broke my promise to you as soon as I made it,' he acknowledged gruffly.

'No, it was me,' she admitted shakily. 'I was going to—was about to——'

'God, I wish you had, Cat,' he groaned. 'I would have liked to give you pleasure.'

She swallowed hard, avoiding his eyes. 'I—I would like to get up now.'

Caleb gently cupped her chin and made her look up at him. 'It isn't wrong to feel desire and pleasure, Cat,' he encouraged softly.

'I know that,' she frowned.

'But you're sorry it happened.' He swung away from her, sitting up to button his shirt. 'I'm not going to be as hypocritical,' he rasped. 'I'm not at all sorry!'

Cat took advantage of his averted gaze to pull on her own clothing. Was she being hypocritical, pretending not to want his lovemaking? She was too confused to know any more, each resolve she made not to let him touch her broken at his slightest show of desire. She didn't recognise herself as the woman who reacted so wantonly in his arms.

'Caleb——'

'Go to bed, little cat,' he instructed gently. 'Dream of me.'

Dream of him. She had done little else since she had met him. Except last night.

And that night, too.

She lay awake for a long time in the huge four-poster bed, that and the imaginings she had had of him as a feudal lord earlier in the evening making her sure that Caleb would come to her in her dreams again that night. Instead she was once again the distraught woman in the white nightgown looking in the darkness for her lover. And again he hadn't come to her.

She awoke feeling irritable and frustrated. Not unlike the way she had gone to bed! Her body seemed to have demands of its own, was paying her back for denying it satisfaction the previous night.

Her mood hadn't improved by the time she had showered and dressed in a black woollen skirt and pale green lambswool sweater. She wasn't going to risk making a bad impression on Lucien Steele at the outset by appearing in trousers, conscious of the fact that he might not approve of women wearing trousers.

She was frowning as she walked down the stairs, the frown turning to a scowl as she saw Caleb in conversation with Norm in the reception area. Caleb stiffened, and then turned to look at her, as if he had sensed her presence part-way down the stairs. He didn't take his eyes off her as he said something dismissive to the other man, Norm walking away after giving Cat a brief smile of greeting, a smile she half-heartedly returned.

Why couldn't Caleb have looked at her and dismissed *her* as he had all those mornings ago!

He had walked to the bottom of the stairs now, his arm resting on the bannister as he watched her descent, his eyes warm, a smile of welcome playing about his lips.

'Caleb——'

'Cat,' he cut in with firm indulgence. 'You look beautiful!'

'I——'

He gently pulled her down on to the last step,

his arms about her waist as he held her gently into him. 'Let's say good morning properly,' he groaned, before his mouth came down on hers.

All her irritation evaporated beneath the warmth of his kiss, and with a soft moan of surrender her body curved willingly into his, her arms going about his neck as she returned the caress.

'That's better.' He looked at her with warm dark eyes. 'Good morning, sweetheart,' he said huskily.

'Good morning,' she returned, knowing her cheeks were flushed, her eyes over-bright.

Caleb seemed satisfied with the turmoil he had caused within her, smiling indulgently. 'Feel up to meeting my father now?' he teased.

She didn't feel up to meeting anyone. Her legs felt weak, and she just wanted Caleb to pick her up in his arms and carry her back up the stairs, to his bedroom this time.

'Yes,' she answered huskily.

Caleb laughed softly. 'Don't look so nervous or he'll eat you alive!'

Oh God, not another awe-inspiring Steele! After the way she had just melted into Caleb's arms she didn't think she could cope with it.

'Come on,' he teased, his arm about her shoulders. 'I'll look after you.'

Who was going to protect her from *him*?

There was only one person in the dining room, a man seated at the long table, the thick hair completely silver as his son's would no doubt be one day. In profile Lucien Steele was as formidable as Caleb, still retaining the handsome good looks of his youth that had so captivated the beautiful Sonia Harrison. He looked as if he were still a physically powerful man, and as he turned to look at them Cat saw that his eyes were almost as black as his son's. And she saw something else as she gazed into those dark depths.

They were the eyes of a dying man.

CHAPTER SIX

SHE didn't know what had made such a thought enter her head, those eyes crinkling at the corners now as he smiled in greeting. Cat frowned, searching the lined face for the emotion she had just seen, finding only warm curiosity as he stood up, his brows raised as he saw his son's arm about her shoulders.

How could she have even thought this man was dying!

He was as lean and lithely built as Caleb, his trousers snug-fitting, as was the brown sweater he wore. But for a moment, just a brief moment, she had thought she had seen—no, she must have been mistaken. Lucien Steele's body looked as agile and healthy as Caleb claimed his mind still was.

'Miss Howard.' His accent was as English as his grandson's. 'It is Miss Howard, isn't it?' he added mockingly. 'Or are you a friend of my son's?' He quirked those silver brows again.

Colour darkened her cheeks before she hastily moved from within the circle of Caleb's arm. The last thing she needed was for Lucien Steele to make any more assumptions about Caleb and herself! After what Luke had already told him that would be all too easy!

'No. I mean, yes,' she amended at Caleb's sceptical expression. 'Er—that is——'

'I know what you're trying to say, Miss Howard,' Lucien Steele chuckled softly, looking past her to his son. 'Whatever Luke's other faults you have to admit he showed good taste,' he derided.

Caleb's mouth twisted mockingly. 'Unfortunately, good taste didn't come into it; Cat could have looked like a female wrestler and Luke would still have played his cruel little trick!' he rasped.

His father's eyes narrowed. 'Cruel?' he prompted softly.

'Cruel,' Caleb nodded grimly. 'Cat doesn't need any more pain in her life.'

Lucien Steele turned to her with widely curious eyes, and Cat squirmed a little under that close scrutiny. Just when she thought she couldn't stand it any more he turned back to his son. 'I'll see Miss Howard at four-thirty for tea,' he instructed curtly. 'Enjoy your day, Miss Howard,' he drawled before leaving.

Cat didn't move for several seconds, her breath seeming to be stuck in her throat. Then she gave a ragged sigh as it was released, turning to look at Caleb. 'Thank you.' She gave a weary smile. 'I have a feeling your father *would* have "eaten me alive" if you hadn't been here!'

Caleb grimaced. 'His bark's always been worse than his bite.' He held out a chair at the table for Cat to sit down.

She did so, shuddering slightly. 'I didn't think there could be another man as arrogantly outspoken as you,' she admitted candidly.

Caleb laughed softly. 'You've just met my tutor!'

She had already guessed that, Lucien Steele's hauteur all the more effective because it was hidden behind warm smiles Caleb didn't even try to affect. The author had completely unnerved her.

'Here,' Caleb poured her cup of coffee, adding the milk and spoonful of sugar she usually took.

Cat frowned at the act of intimacy, and yet she knew if she had been the one to pour his coffee that she would have known he took it black and unsweetened. She tried to remember how Harry took his coffee—and couldn't.

'I can serve myself, thank you,' she snapped, as Caleb would have put bacon and eggs down in front of her from the serving dishes on the side-table.

He gave her a narrow-eyed look. 'I've done it now,' he grated at her rebellious expression.

Green eyes warred with black. 'I don't like bacon *or* eggs,' she lied.

Irritation darkened his brow as he put the plate down at his own place. 'Then just tell me what you do like for breakfast and I'll get it for you!' he rasped.

Cat stared down at the white tablecloth in front of her. What she liked! She *liked* this man's arms around her, the feel of his lips against hers, the warm way he was starting to look at her. What she *didn't* like was liking those things!

'I'm not hungry.' This time she didn't lie; her appetite had completely deserted her. Only last night as she climbed into bed she had tried to remember the exact shade of blue of Harry's eyes, only to have them superseded by un-fathomable black orbs. She was starting to forget Harry, and it was all this man's fault!

'I think I'd like to work this morning if you——'

'We're going skiing,' he told her flatly, the food in front of him remaining untouched.

'I told you, I can't ski——'

'And I told you you can learn,' he bit out.

'I don't want to,' she snapped.

Cruelly thinned lips twisted with displeasure. 'I would advise you to remember that you're a guest here,' he threatened softly.

'And if I don't behave myself you'll ask me to leave!' her eyes flashed.

'No——'

'I think *yes*!' She stood up. 'I don't give out bedroom favours to keep my informant sweet!' she told him with distaste.

'Be quiet, you little fool!' Caleb stood up, too, his expression fierce. 'You don't know what you're talking about!'

'I *know*,' she assured him heatedly.

'Damn you, Cat,' he grated harshly. 'You——' He broke off as the door was suddenly opened.

'Oops!' An embarrassed looking Norm had become the object of Caleb's glitteringly angry gaze the instant he showed himself to be the intruder. 'I was going to join you for breakfast,' he told them awkwardly, the tension between Cat and Caleb so thick it could almost be touched. 'But I can always come back later.' Once you've left, he mentally seemed to add.

'No.' Cat stopped him as he turned to leave, deeply regretting that he should have had to walk in on yet another argument between herself and Caleb. 'I'll go——'

'No, I will,' Caleb rasped coldly. 'I have some things to do before we go out.'

Cat knew that the last was a warning that the two of them were still going skiing today, and she sat down shakily as the door was slammed behind him. What was *happening* to her? She didn't even particularly like Caleb, and yet he was slowly pushing all the memories she had of Harry from her mind. Except one. She still remembered the way she had loved him and he had loved her. And those feelings had no resemblance to the way she and Caleb felt about each other.

She felt a little better as she raised her head to smile at Norm. 'Come and sit down,' she invited smoothly. 'Caleb and I were just having our daily dispute.' She tried to make light of the heated argument he had interrupted.

'Who won?' he derided, sitting down beside the bacon and eggs Caleb hadn't touched.

She gave a rueful smile. 'Guess!'

He laughed softly. 'What did you make of Lucien?' he asked curiously.

'Like son, like father,' she misquoted drily.

Norm nodded. 'They're alike all right,' he grinned.

'And you like both of them immensely.'

'Immensely,' he teasingly mimicked her English accent. 'And so do you.'

'Has any woman ever *liked* Caleb?' she

ridiculed the lukewarm emotion in connection with that arrogant man.

'You could be right,' Norm acknowledged slowly. 'But you feel something for him.'

Did she? He was a torment and a tease, but yes, she felt something for him. The question was, what was it?

She watched him surreptitiously as he drove the Range Rover towards Aviemore and the Cairngorm mountains. He was still furiously angry with her for the way she had acted at breakfast. She had known that from the moment he brought Norm's ski-suit to her at her bedroom and instructed her to put it on; had been even more convinced of it as they made the drive in total silence, his mouth a thin line, his eyes harshly narrowed.

Finally she had had enough. 'If I apologise will you stop sulking?' she cajoled.

Black eyes flashed her an angry glare. 'I do not sulk!'

At that moment he was doing exactly that, reminding Cat of a disgruntled little boy who couldn't get his own way. She had difficulty holding back her smile. 'Caleb, I am sorry.'

'For what?' he bit out. 'I only poured you a cup of coffee, and put you some breakfast on a plate!'

Her humour faded as her eyes took on a haunted look. 'Maybe if I could explain——'

'I wish someone would,' he rasped tightly. 'One minute we were sharing a joke about the similarity between my father and me and the next you were snapping my head off for God knows what!'

She closed her eyes, knowing he had a right to be angry and confused. 'It was the coffee.' She kept her eyes closed, although she sensed his startled look. 'I suddenly realised——' She swallowed hard, knowing she owed him this explanation, even though it was painful to make. 'You take your coffee black and unsweetened?' she said with a sigh.

'Yes,' he confirmed impatiently, as if he didn't understand what they had to do with anything.

'And you know I take a little milk and one spoonful of sugar,' she said sadly. 'It made me realise I no longer remembered how Harry took his coffee. I know it must seem silly, but——'

'No.' His hand covered both of hers as they moved restlessly on her lap. 'It isn't silly,' he assured her huskily. 'And I understand now.'

She looked at him with shadowed eyes. 'You do?' she frowned.

'Yes.' He turned to give her a gentle smile. 'Thank you for explaining to me.'

He didn't say any more, and neither did she, the silence between them companionable now.

Cat's eyes began to sparkle in anticipation as the mountains that could be seen in the distance from the Steele home took on their proper proportions once they had driven through the pretty little town of Aviemore, the snow heavier the nearer they got to the mountains, the road that went up to the skiing area packed at the sides with cleared snow.

Dozens of cars were parked in the area before

the ski-lodge, laughing happy people dressed similarly to Cat and Caleb getting out of their vehicles to unstrap their skis from roof-racks, boot-racks, inside cars and trucks, from any place they had managed to secure them. With their ski-boots on and their skis thrown over their shoulders they looked very professional.

'Caleb, I don't think I——'

'You'll love it,' he predicted, before climbing out of the Range Rover, his own navy blue ski-suit showing the lithe perfection of his body.

Cat climbed out more reluctantly, following him round to the back of the vehicle. 'I'll make a fool of myself,' she grimaced.

'And what's wrong with making a fool of yourself now and then?' He pulled the skis and poles easily out on to the packed snow beneath their feet.

'That's easy for you to say,' she snapped crossly. 'You've never done it!'

He looked round at her in stunned surprise, frowning slightly before he began to chuckle. 'You know, I think you're right. Except maybe once,' he sobered. 'When I mistook the motives of the honey-blonde cat curled up in my bed!'

'That wasn't your fault,' she exonerated him of all blame.

'No, it wasn't,' he acknowledged hardly. 'But I seem to have made an idiot of myself several more times over the same cat the last few weeks. So one more time isn't going to make much difference,' he said mockingly, before moving determinedly towards her.

'Caleb!'

'What?' His eyes were dark with desire as he took her in his arms.

'We're in a public car park!' As if to prove her panicked protest a car whooshed past them looking for a parking space further up.

'So?' he murmured close to her lips.

'So I don't go in for displays!'

Caleb laughed softly. 'Neither do I—usually.' His mouth claimed hers in a kiss that wouldn't be denied, running his tongue moistly along the edge of her lower lip, but not entering the warm cavern beneath.

Cat forgot where they were, no longer heard the laughing voices of the people around them as her arms shyly moved up around his neck and she returned the kiss.

Caleb was the one to finally end the fiery caress. 'I think we had better go skiing,' he said ruefully as he put her away from him.

'Don't you mean falling?' A disgruntled Cat followed in his wake, happy to let him carry both pairs of skis while she clumsily tried to keep her balance in Norm's cumbersome ski-boots.

He turned to give her a grin. 'Do you know what I like about you the most?'

Colour darkened her cheeks. 'Caleb!' She looked about them self-consciously to see if anyone had heard his remark.

He gave a throaty chuckle. 'Catherine Howard,' he reproved with amusement, 'I was referring to the fact that you have the ability to make me laugh.'

'Oh good,' she said with sarcasm, holding on to the wall of the building as they walked up the steps beside the lodge towards the ski-lifts, wondering how Caleb managed to make the task look so damned easy. *Everyone* else made it look easy!

Caleb stopped to wait for her, amusement still lurking in the dark eyes as she panted up the steps. 'It's a wonderful gift, Cat,' he chided. 'People enjoy just being around you.'

She refused to meet his gaze in case he should see the unexpected tears of sentiment appear in her eyes. 'In that case you're really going to enjoy the next couple of hours!' she deliberately misunderstood him.

'Would you prefer to have a professional teacher?' He took pity on her awkwardness.

She had no doubt that this man ski'd well enough to have been a professional; he seemed to do everything well. 'Why let a complete stranger have the benefit of all that amusement?' she derided.

'Cat——'

'Caleb, I really don't mind.' She let him see the laughter in her eyes. 'If you don't.'

'I'll enjoy teaching you to ski,' he assured her.

And in the next hour or so Cat learnt why he enjoyed it! 'Teaching her to ski' gave Caleb ample opportunity to touch her and caress her as he demonstrated the movements she should make with her body, and then helped her up as she fell flat on her bottom. After the embarrassment of the first few falls Cat found the whole thing hilarious, falling laughingly into Caleb's waiting arms.

They had taken the chair-lift half-way up the

mountain, carrying their skis with them, for
which Cat was very grateful; all the ski-lifts she
had seen on television always had the skiers
getting on and off with their skis firmly fixed to
their boots. The view when they got off was
wonderful, the crisp air exhilarating, and if she
didn't make too much of a success of her first
day's skiing she didn't particularly care.

'That's enough for today,' Caleb decided
after almost two hours. 'You're getting cold and
tired.'

She hadn't thought he had noticed, and she
hadn't liked to say when they were having such a
good time. She should have known Caleb would
know exactly how she was feeling!

'Why don't you go back up and have a nice
long run down from the top?' she suggested once
he had brought her down on the chair-lift. 'It
can't have been much fun just teaching me. I
know you enjoyed it,' she mocked as he went to
protest, 'but I'm sure you could give most of the
people here a lesson on how it should be done!'
He moved about on his skies as if he were born to
them and not as if they were a mortal enemy that
kept sliding away from him as hers did.

'You're cold——'

'If you give me the keys I can let myself into
the Range Rover.'

He was tempted, it was there in the wistful
expression of his eyes.

'Please,' she encouraged.

'If you're sure . . .?'

'I wouldn't have suggested it if I weren't,' she
teased.

'OK.' He got the Range Rover's keys out of his pocket. 'I won't be long,' he promised, kissing her swiftly on the mouth before getting back on the chair-lift.

Cat had no intention of returning to the Range Rover without him, moving to the shelter of the lodge to watch Caleb descend. He moved easily and gracefully, barely using the poles he carried, making the sport look easy, when Cat knew very well that it wasn't. She wasn't the only one admiring him, several other people turning to watch him. And why not? He looked as if he ought to have been a professional.

Several people congratulated him as he ski'd down the small slope to the lodge, his eyes widening as he saw Cat waiting for him.

'I just wanted to see how it should be done,' she teased lightly.

'If I'd known you were watching I would have done a couple of fancy turns.' He took off his skis to walk along beside her.

No, he wouldn't, because he wasn't the exhibitionist type, and they both knew it. He wasn't showy or self-inflated, he was just confident in what he did.

'Lunch, I think,' he suggested on the drive back down to Aviemore.

Cat thought lunch sounded a good idea as she suddenly realized how hungry she was.

Caleb parked the Range Rover in Aviemore station, leaving Cat to pull on her walking boots while he went to get the display ticket. Aviemore wasn't a big place, but it had several nice shops, and Cat entered a toy shop to buy one of the space toys that were such a hit with children at the moment.

'A secret hobby?' Caleb mocked once they emerged on to the street again.

'Hardly,' she returned drily. 'My nephew is fascinated by them at the moment.'

'Nephew?' he echoed sharply. 'You said you didn't have a brother.'

'I don't,' she derided.

'But a nephew——'

'Means that I have a sibling,' she mocked. 'Really, Caleb, I didn't think you were a chauvinist,' she taunted. 'Vikki is like a sister to me, but—which reminds me.' Her eyes were wide. 'Could I telephone her later to let her know I'm all right? She was sure you were going to be here this weekend; I'm sure she would like to know she was right,' she grimaced.

'By all means call your friend,' he nodded. 'Vikki is like a sister to you, but——?' he prompted.

She smiled. 'I have the bona fide kind. Susan is ten years older than me, and my nephew Josh is eight.'

Caleb didn't return her smile, as she had thought he would, but frowned darkly. 'I know very little about you really, do I?' he muttered, as if the realisation deeply displeased him.

'There's no reason why you should——'

'There's every reason,' he grated. 'Over lunch you can tell me your life story, from the moment the doctor slapped your bottom.'

'In the first place you'll be bored,' she warned him. 'And in the second,' she grimaced, 'the doctor didn't need to slap my bottom; I was so indignant at being born that I promptly disgraced myself all down the front of his nice green robe. So my mother tells me,' she added ruefully.

Caleb was so busy laughing at her childhood and adolescent antics that neither of them showed too much interest in the hamburgers they had ordered for lunch. He was also far from bored, Cat noted with satisfaction.

'Now it's your turn,' she invited as she ate her banana split for dessert.

He sobered instantly, and Cat regretted wiping the laughter from his eyes. 'It was nothing like the fun you had growing up,' he bit out, a faraway look in his eyes.

'It must have been fascinating though,' she prompted. 'Meeting all those film stars.'

'There's really nothing fascinating about a lot of insecure people trying to lose themselves behind images other people create for them,' he rasped. 'At least when my mother was alive there was some degree of normality to our lives, but after she died I practically grew up on the sets of the films my father had written, in the middle of false images and false values. I still lived in that world of make-believe when I met Deanna; I didn't realise that what she really wanted was my father to write parts for her in his films so that she could be what she had always wanted to be, a "star"!' Bitterness iced his eyes. 'I didn't want a wife that wanted to be away from Luke and me more than she was with us, so I gave her an ultimatum. She left, because by that time she had the stardom she wanted. It was then that I decided Luke wasn't going to grow up in that fantasy world the way I had.'

'That was why he went to live with his grandfather,' Cat realized.

'Yes,' he grated.

'But you let that fantasy world continue to run your own life,' she frowned.

'No,' he scorned. '*I* now run that fantasy world.' His mouth twisted. 'I prefer it that way. And Luke was happy living with his grandfather.'

But Caleb had lost out on so much, had lost that closeness with his son that was so important.

'Before you talk to my father this afternoon there's something I think you should know,' he bit out.

Oh God! She hadn't been right about what she had seen in his eyes this morning, had she?

Caleb drew in a ragged breath. 'When I once told you Lucien is more lucid than a lot of men half his age I spoke the truth,' he said slowly. 'Most of the time he is,' he added softly. 'But sometimes—not very often,' he swiftly assured her, 'he wanders. And what he says during those times doesn't make much sense.' He looked at her intently, trying to gauge her reaction to what he had just told her.

Cat frowned. 'Is that why you didn't want me to meet him?'

'Yes,' he sighed.

Her hand lightly touched his across the table. 'A lot of elderly people wander off into their past, Caleb,' she reassured him. 'It doesn't detract from their intelligence. And your father is obviously still a very talented man.'

He nodded abruptly. 'But some of the things he says when he wanders aren't believable—or pleasant.'

She gave him an understanding smile. 'I'm not here to write about your father as he is now, Caleb; I'm sure his work does that for him. I only want to know about his marriage to your mother.'

He gave another deep sigh. 'Well, you can't say I didn't warn you.'

Cat went out of her way to make him laugh again on the drive back to the house, knew it had taken a lot of courage for him to talk about his father the way he had. But Vikki's grandmother had always been one to live in the past, the stories of her youth fascinating. She was sure she could cope with Lucien Steele's lapses.

The two of them were laughing companionably together over her efforts at skiing as they entered the Steele house.

'Well, well, well,' mocked a contemptuous voice. 'And here was I thinking you were sure to be at each others' throats by now.'

All of the humour left Cat's flushed face as she turned to face their tormentor as he supported himself on short arm crutches, his broken leg still in plaster. Luke Steele!

CHAPTER SEVEN

HE looked at them both with coldly derisive eyes, that insolent gaze boldly sweeping over Cat's wind-tousled appearance before moving to the narrow-eyed man at her side, his own mouth tightening as he recognised that his father's indulgent humour of a few moments ago had been completely wiped out as he looked at *him*.

'What the hell are you doing here?' Caleb demanded impatiently.

Luke didn't blink an eyelid in the face of his father's displeasure, his expression remaining insolent. 'I live here,' he bit out, his gaze sliding once again to Cat. 'Or has that changed in the last two days?' he challenged.

Cat felt rather than saw Caleb's tension increase, and she wished there were something she could do to help the situation between this angry man and his defiant son. But she knew she couldn't, that it was none of her business. Luke was only using her as a stick to beat his father with, and when Caleb no longer rose to the bait, he would move on to something else that put his father on the defensive.

'You know damn well it hasn't,' Caleb rasped. 'But it's been so long since you came here that— how *did* you get here?' he frowned.

'I instructed your pilot and he brought me,' Luke derided.

His father's mouth thinned. 'I'm sure your grandfather was surprised to see you.'

'Not particularly,' Luke dismissed carelessly. 'I rang him last night and told him I was thinking of coming up; he thought it was a good idea.'

No emotion showed in Caleb's eyes at this last disclosure, and yet Cat knew he was hurt that Luke had chosen to talk to his grandfather and not to him. They had lost so much, this father and son!

'And talking of grandfather,' Luke drawled, cold blue eyes once more turning on Cat, 'I'm afraid my arrival has tired him out, so he doesn't feel up to your little chat this afternoon now. You'll just have to be satisfied with my father until tomorrow morning.' He gave a scornful look that seemed to encompass them both. 'Although that doesn't seem to have bothered you so far.'

Caleb's hands clenched into fists at his sides, his eyes glacial. 'You will re-phrase that last statement,' he ordered through gritted teeth.

'About it bothering her?' Luke taunted. 'But I can't see anything——'

'No, damn it!' his father bit out furiously. 'I realise this may be a little difficult for you to do,' he rasped, 'but you'll treat Cat with respect!'

Cat swallowed hard at again becoming the focus of contention between these two men. 'Caleb, it doesn't mat——'

'Apologise for your insinuation,' Caleb coldly instructed Luke, ignoring Cat's dismissal.

'Why?' his son challenged.

'Haven't you done her enough harm already?' Caleb accused icily.

Luke's eyes widened. 'My God,' he taunted. 'I'm not going to be presented with a stepmother at this stage in my life, am I?'

All colour drained from Cat's cheeks, leaving her deathly white, putting out a hand to stop him as Caleb would have swung a punch at his son. 'That isn't going to help, Caleb,' she pleaded.

'You mean it's true?' Luke scorned. 'Good God, I thought you had more sense than to let yourself be caught by a woman *I* put in your bed!'

'Caleb, remember his leg!' she shouted as this time it seemed he would go ahead with striking his son.

He stopped himself with effort, standing only inches from Luke now, the taller by a couple of inches. 'You are going to apologise to Cat,' he told the younger man with deadly calm.

The blue eyes widened only fractionally as Luke assessed his father's mood, long timeless seconds passing before he gave a barely perceptible shrug of his shoulders. 'What am I apologising for?' he sighed. 'The fact that she's now your mistress, or the fact that I know about it?'

'Caleb, *no*!' She managed to stop him as once again he would have hit his son, looking at Luke with pitying eyes. 'You know, by the time you grow up there could be no one around to impress!'

His cheeks reddened. 'I don't have to take that from my father's——'

'Friend,' she calmly substituted for the crude word she was sure he had been going to use, sure that if he had it would have pushed Caleb too far, and that this time she wouldn't be able to stop him. 'Now I don't know why you're so angry at your father, Luke, that's between the two of you, but I won't be brought into it. Do you understand?' she prompted hardly.

'I don't——'

'Luke, the condition you're in at the moment even *I* could knock you to the ground,' she warned. 'I'd probably enjoy it, too, but you would look a little foolish.'

He drew in an angry breath. 'All right, I apologise,' he said flatly—and without the least shred of sincerity.

'That isn't——'

'It's really all right, Caleb.' She turned to give him a tight smile. 'I think if you don't mind I'll go and make my telephone call now.'

'Cat!'

She turned at the foot of the stairs, pain in her eyes as she looked at Caleb.

Ignoring his son completely he walked over to her, gently touching her cheek. 'You'll come down to dinner?' he prompted.

She knew he must have guessed that she had intended staying in her room. She had no doubt Lucien Steele would once again not be present for the meal, not if he didn't feel up to seeing her now, and as Norm didn't seem to be much help during these encounters she didn't relish the thought of finding herself caught in the middle of these two men again.

'Don't worry, Miss Howard,' Luke drawled at her hesitation. 'I'm always in a more pleasant mood once I've eaten.'

Her eyes flashed as she glared at him. 'You must have a very inflated ego if you think your mood is of the least interest to me,' she told him dismissively. 'I was merely regretting the fact that your father and I wouldn't be alone tonight as we were yesterday.' She watched the angry flush darken his cheeks before turning to Caleb with triumphant warmth. 'I wouldn't dream of not joining you for dinner,' she assured him.

He smiled at her. 'I'll look forward to it——'

'If this is going to run like a scene from *Romeo and Juliet* I think I'll go out into the garden and throw up!' Luke stormed awkwardly out the front door.

The humour instantly left Caleb's eyes to be replaced by a pained frown. 'I'm sorry you had to be caught in the middle of that,' he rasped darkly. 'I can assure you it wasn't personal.'

'I know that.' She squeezed his arm understandingly. 'Is he always so—angry?'

'Most of the time,' Caleb nodded sadly.

'Have you ever tried talking to him about your reasons for sending him to his grandfather fifteen years ago?' she prompted gently.

His mouth tightened. 'If you think that's the reason he's like he is then let me assure you it isn't.' He shook his head. 'Until a few years ago we were quite close.'

'What happened?' she frowned.

'Are you asking as my "friend" or as a reporter?' he drawled.

'I've told you more times than I care to think about, I am not that type of reporter!'

'Then, who knows?' His gaze was suddenly

evasive as he shrugged dismissively. 'I love my son, Cat, but I can't protect him from everything.'

'Then something is troubling him?'

His expression darkened and he was suddenly very remote. 'Only the usual pains of growing up,' he bit out abruptly, stepping back. 'He'll get over it, we all do.'

His voice lacked sincerity, his gaze still evasive, and Cat wisely decided it was really none of her business as she ran lightly up the stairs.

A glance out of the bedroom window showed Luke wasn't 'throwing up' in the garden at all but clumping around it on his crutches, oblivious to the falling snow. He looked lonely and alone, and more than a little lost with his guard down.

Cat turned away, knowing he wouldn't welcome her intrusive curiosity if he should glance up and see her watching him. It wasn't just the painful process of growing up that was bothering him, she was sure of it.

'How are you? *Where* are you?' Vikki cried excitedly a few minutes later as soon as Cat had identified herself on the phone. 'Is Caleb there? What's Lucien Steele like? Do you——'

'Will you slow down?' Cat laughed teasingly. 'You aren't giving me time to answer you!'

'Oh. Oh no,' Vikki conceded ruefully. 'Well?' she prompted impatiently.

'I'm fine. Caleb is here. Mr Steele seems very nice,' she answered drily.

'And you aren't going to say where you are,' Vikki guessed as she omitted to answer that question.

'No, I——' She broke off as there was a strange noise on the line. 'Vikki? Are you still there?'

'I was just wondering the same about you,' her friend returned clearly. 'It sounded as if we were cut off,' she added in a puzzled voice.

Or someone had put down an extension! God, didn't Caleb know her well enough, trust her enough by now, to realise she wouldn't betray that confidence? 'The line seems to be all right now,' she bit out tautly.

'Yes,' Vikki still sounded puzzled, and then she seemed to dismiss the faulty line. 'Have you done your interview yet?'

'Tomorrow,' she said abruptly, still angry at having her call listened in on. Because there could be no other explanation for what she had heard.

'And has Caleb succeeded in seducing you yet?' Vikki teased.

'Isn't that presuming that he's trying to?' she returned lightly.

'I *know* he's trying to,' Vikki mocked.

Had he succeeded? Until he had shut her out concerning his son, and that strange clicking sound on the phone just now, she would have said she was definitely falling under the magnetism of his charm and seduction. But it had been a fragile emotion at best, and his distrust of her had destroyed it.

'Maybe,' she avoided.

'But it isn't working.' Vikki sounded disappointed.

'Anyone would think you were trying to get rid of me,' she derided.

'Then anyone would be wrong,' Vikki instantly denied. 'I'm just waiting to hear your opinion on lust before trying it myself!'

They both laughed at that. Vikki's long-term relationship with Sam was platonic to say the least.

Cat didn't hesitate, after ringing off a short time later, in going downstairs to look for Caleb, finding him in what she had been informed by the maid was 'the master's study', he and Norm pouring over some papers on his desk.

Norm took one look at her stormy face and straightened. 'I think this is where I came in,' he drawled derisively.

Caleb frowned across at her, his eyes narrowing. 'Except nothing happened in either Cat's or my bed last night,' he rasped slowly.

'I'll come back later,' Norm said quickly, closing the door behind him.

'How could you?' Cat instantly accused. 'How *dare* you?' she blazed. 'What did you think I was doing, telephoning a newspaper and telling them where your father is?' she added digustedly. 'I thought you trusted me——'

'I do,' he cut in quietly, standing up to pull out a chair for her in front of his desk. 'Sit down and tell me what's wrong.'

'You know what's wrong,' she spluttered indignantly, ignoring the chair, having no intention of putting herself at such a disadvantage by sitting when he was standing. 'I *asked* you if I could call Vikki. You had only to say if you minded——'

'But I didn't. And I don't.' He frowned at her vehemence.

'Only because you *know* I haven't told Vikki where we are,' she snapped.

'Cat——'

'If listening to other people's conversations is part of "your world" then I'm glad I don't belong to it!'

'Someone *listened* in on your conversation to Vikki?' he realised slowly.

She gave him a scathing look. 'Don't try to pretend it wasn't you——'

'But it wasn't,' he cut in coldly. 'And if we're making accusations about trusting people . . .' he added icily.

She looked at him searchingly, the chill of his eyes, the firm anger of his mouth. 'It wasn't you,' she sighed regretfully. 'But if not you, who— Luke?' she questioned dazedly, remembering that the younger man had been coming towards the house before she made her telephone call. 'Do you think it was him?' she grimaced.

'Perhaps.' He gave a cold inclination of his head. 'Unless you imagined it?'

The laughing companion of the day had gone, and in his place the arrogant stranger of that first morning. Cat felt regret for that; she had liked that other Caleb. 'I didn't imagine it,' she said flatly. 'And I'm sorry if I was mistaken about the identity of the person that did it.'

She wasn't easily forgiven, Caleb's expression not softening in the slightest. 'I'll talk to Luke about it,' he rasped. 'Although I wouldn't expect an apology from him,' he added. 'He very rarely apologises for his behaviour.'

'Caleb——'

'If that's all, Cat.' He cut across her pleading tone. 'I have some work to do.'

She shouldn't have just assumed the eaves-dropper was him, she knew that now. He may have seemed the obvious choice at the time, but the more she thought about it the more she realised she should have known it wouldn't be him; he hadn't needed to have her brought here in the first place, could have ignored his father's invitation to her or just told his father she had refused, but he had obviously trusted her enough not to do either of those things.

She put both her hands on his arm. 'I really am sorry.' Green eyes pleaded with remote black ones. 'I was just so angry——'

'With perfect right.' Some of the tension left his body. 'As I made it clear at the onset that I didn't approve of your visit here perhaps you felt it could be no one else but me. But surely you must have realised I've changed my mind about you since you arrived?' He allowed her briefly to see the pain in his eyes.

She had hurt him, really hurt him, with her accusation, and with good reason! 'Caleb, please don't be angry with me——'

'Angry with you?' he repeated harshy. 'I've opened up to you more than any other woman for a very long time only to be met with suspicion and rejection; why the hell should I be angry?'

She winced at the truth of his words, knew that today the coldly remote Caleb Steele had been absent, and in his place had been an indulgent lover. And she had liked that other Caleb. Too much? Was she deliberately trying to push him

away before he got too close? Wasn't it already
too late for that, hadn't she come to care for him
in spite of herself?

'Cat?'

She focused on him with an effort, realising her
hands were still on his arm, stepping back self-
consciously, her expression apprehensive.

His eyes narrowed. 'Another rejection,' he
rasped, drawing in a ragged breath. 'Hell, why
not? They're more effective than a cold shower!'

She had hurt him again, she, who didn't want to
hurt anyone. She had just wanted to live her life
quietly, enjoy her friends; how had she got into this
mess? Why did Caleb keep forcing his feelings on
her when he knew how she felt about them!

'I—I think I'll go and have a soak in the bath,'
she told him woodenly. 'My legs are starting to
stiffen up,' she added lightly, although there was
no answering softening to his features.

'Skiing will do that to you every time,' he bit
out nastily.

She frowned her confusion with his aggression.

'One day, Cat,' he ground out fiercely, 'and
you may consider it as far away as hell freezing
over!—I'm going to make your body ache from
making love with me!'

She gasped her indignation at the claim. 'You
were right, Caleb, it *is* as far away as hell freezing
over!' she told him forcefully before spinning on
her heel and running from the room.

She didn't stop running until she reached her
bedroom, although she knew Caleb hadn't come in
pursuit of her. It wasn't him she was running
from, but her own imaginings! Although they

weren't all dreams and imaginings now, her breasts had ached and throbbed from Caleb's ministrations after she left him last night. Would her whole body know that pleasurable ache if he made love to her completely? She daren't even allow herself to think about it!

Keeping thoughts of Caleb firmly at bay she ran herself a bath, liberally adding some of the perfumed bubble-bath that she found in the cabinet over the sink, taking a book with her as she gratefully sank down into the water, intending to have a long soak while the heat of the water eased her aches and pains.

It didn't seem as if she had been in the bath any time at all before the door was swung wide open with a loud crash, Luke Steele standing in the doorway supported on his crutches.

Cat instinctively dropped the book she was reading down on to her breasts, grateful for the bubbles left floating on the water to hide the rest of her body. 'How dare you?' she gasped. 'What do you think you're doing bursting in here?'

'Looking at you,' he drawled. 'Don't worry, I've done it before. Of course, that time dear old Daddy was almost lying on top of you, but——'

'What do you want, Luke?' she demanded furiously, colour heightening her cheeks. How dare he just walk in here uninvited!

He shrugged, unconcerned with her obvious outrage. 'Dad says you didn't like having your phone call listened in on.' He admitted he had been the eavesdropper without a shred of guilt attached to it. 'He seemed to think I owe you an apology.'

'Well now you owe me two!' Her eyes flashed angrily as she kept the book pressed against her breasts.

He arched mocking brows. 'For walking in on you when you're having a bath?' he scorned. 'Good God, woman, I can't do much about your nakedness in my condition.' He looked down pointedly at the plaster on his leg. 'You're acting like some damned—my God,' he breathed slowly as the thought occurred to him, looking at her flushed cheeks with narrowed eyes. 'I don't believe it,' he finally derided. 'You can't be!'

Cat glared at him resentfully. 'Would you get out of here!'

'A virgin,' he looked at her wonderingly. 'Dad has the hots for a virgin!' he mocked. 'Even my mother couldn't claim to be that when he married her!'

'From all accounts she was a lot of other things, though,' Cat snapped—and instantly regretted her bitchiness. She was angry and upset, but that was no reason to be disparaging about a woman she didn't even know. 'I'm sorry,' she said abruptly. 'I shouldn't have said that. Please don't think it was anything your father said——'

'Don't apologise, Miss Howard,' Luke drawled. 'Even though my mother is on her fifth husband my father never tells people of the bitch she was and is, so please don't think that I believe my father was your informant. My mother is a famous actress, everything she does is news—and she makes sure that it is,' he added derisively. 'I just can't believe Dad would get himself involved with such an innocent as you.' He shook his head wonderingly.

'Your father isn't involved with me,' she told him firmly. 'And might I remind you that neither of us had any choice about the night I spent in his bed!'

Luke looked at her consideringly, from the flyaway blonde hair secured in a single braid at the moment, the face without make-up, over creamy shoulders, down to the spot where the top of her breasts met the water. 'You don't look like a virgin——'

'We don't come with a label attached!' she snapped impatiently.

'There's nothing—odd about you, is there?' he asked curiously.

Her eyes flashed. 'Nothing that punching you in the mouth wouldn't cure!'

'Then why haven't you ever had a lover?' He frowned his puzzlement.

'Is it compulsory?' she challenged heatedly.

'When a woman is as beautiful as you are, yes.'

She blushed at the statement, knowing it had been too bluntly made not to be sincere. 'Well, I haven't,' she dismissed. 'And as my bath water is getting cold . . .' she added pointedly.

'Don't mind me,' he drawled.

'Luke!' she warned. 'You've had your fun,' she bit out, 'but don't push me too far or I might start asking a few personal questions of my own.'

The amusement faded from his eyes as his expression became guarded. 'What do you mean?'

She sighed. 'It doesn't matter,' she shook her head wearily.

'I want to know what you meant,' he said forcefully.

'Luke, please,' she sighed again. 'I spoke out of turn, please forget it.'

For a moment longer he looked rebellious, and then he gave an abrupt nod of his head. 'I take it the fact that I listened to your phone call will also be forgotten?' he challenged.

'As soon as you tell me why you felt the need to bother,' she gave a tight smile.

He shrugged. 'I was interested in who you were telephoning, wondered if you had a lover. As soon as I realised it was another woman you were talking to I rang off.'

'Are you a voyeur?'

'I listened, Cat, I didn't look,' he rasped. 'I just wondered what Dad would say to you having another man in your life.'

'Nothing,' she said abruptly. 'I wish you would get it through your head that there is nothing between your father and myself.'

'I witnessed the Romeo and Juliet scene, remember,' he said disgustedly.

'I believe your father is a little old for Romeo,' she derided.

Luke smiled. 'So you do have a sense of humour after all.'

'When something is genuinely funny and not just cruel,' she told him pointedly.

'A lot of women would have envied you that night,' he dismissed. 'Besides, you got your interview in the end, didn't you?'

Yes, she had got her interview, although it was taking until the last day of her stay here to get it.

She wondered if what she was going through with Caleb and Luke was worth it!

Lucien Steele was once again absent from the dinner table that evening, while Norm opted to have his dinner on a tray in his room while he did some work, and Cat sat between Luke and Caleb as if waiting for a time-bomb to go off. The final tick could be heard as she poured them all coffee in the lounge after their meal.

'Did the book dry out OK?'

Cat looked up to find Luke was talking to her. 'Book?' she repeated in a puzzled voice, suddenly wary of his jovial politeness after he had virtually ignored her throughout the meal.

'The one you were reading in the bath when we talked earlier,' he explained, with all the innocence of a child discussing the flavours of ice-cream!

It took all of her courage to turn and look at Caleb, and once she had she wished she hadn't. He had gone rigidly still, his mouth a thin angry line, his cold gaze raking over Cat and Luke, before it finally came to rest on—Cat! She swallowed hard, knowing Luke's deliberate attempt to cause trouble had once again succeeded.

'You invited my son in for a *chat* while you were taking your bath?' he demanded furiously.

'No, I——'

He stood up forcefully. 'If I'd known your taste still ran for boys I wouldn't have bothered you,' he rasped coldly.

'Caleb, you——'

'He isn't Harry, Cat,' he told her cruelly. 'And

closing your eyes and wishing he were will never make it so!' He stormed from the room.

'Who is Harry?'

Cat turned furiously to Luke Steele, striding across the room to slap him powerfully across the cheek.

CHAPTER EIGHT

SHE glared down at Luke as he put a hand up to the cheek she had just struck, red welts already beginning to show against his pale skin. 'Who was Harry?' she repeated furiously. 'He's a man whose boots you aren't even fit to lick!'

'A saint, is he?' Luke drawled. 'What a bore.'

Cat was breathing heavily, sick of this young man's acts of cruelty and destruction, sick of the self-pity that he thought gave him the right to commit those acts, of the belief he seemed to have that he was the only one to have ever received an unfair kick from life. Most of all, she was sick of *him*.

'For all I know he could be exactly that,' she bit out forcefully.

'A bore or a saint?' Luke derided.

'A saint!' Her eyes flashed a warning he was too self-centred to see. 'He was good and kind, hated to have to hurt anyone.'

'You should have married such a paragon,' Luke scorned.

'I would have done,' she assured him with dislike.

'But he found you too much of a bore, hmm?' Luke taunted.

'He loved me as much as I loved him!'

'Obviously not enough to make it legal,' he drawled. 'Now I——' He broke off, looking

sharply at Cat, at the paleness of her face and the
fire in her eyes. 'You keep talking about him in
the past tense . . .' he realised. 'Cat, is he——?'

'Dead?' she finished harshly. 'Yes, Harry died.
On our wedding day.' She watched dispassionately as Luke flinched, his face even paler. 'He
was nineteen years old, a wonderful loving man,
and I loved him. Now I don't know what makes
you think you have some God-given right to the
monopoly on misery and despair, but let me tell
you it isn't yours; I have more than my fair
share!' she told him shakily.

His eyes were dark bottomless pools in his
white face. 'How did you survive all that?' he
asked in a numbed voice.

'I had no choice,' she rasped. 'I wasn't in the
car with Harry when he crashed.'

'I—oh God,' Luke stumbled to his feet with
the help of his crutches. 'Excuse me.' He couldn't
look at her. 'I—I have to go. I need——' He
hurried as best he could from the room.

Cat dropped down weakly on to a chair. She
had never before lost her temper in that way over
Harry's death. She had felt despair, impatience,
bleakness, and finally acceptance. But just now
she had been so angry.

She hadn't meant to say those cruel things to
Luke, to hurt him any more than he was already
hurting, she just hadn't been able to stop herself.
Shame washed over her for inflicting such a
rebuke on him. His pain was *now*, not five years
old, and whatever it was it was tearing him apart
as much as losing Harry had her.

She had to find Luke, explain——

'Have Mr Caleb and Master Luke finished their coffee?' A puzzled Mrs McDonald looked down at the three untouched cups of coffee that sat on the tray.

'Er—Luke didn't feel too well, and—and Caleb helped him up to his room,' she invented lamely. 'Could you tell me which bedroom is Luke's?' she enquired innocently. 'I just want to check that he's all right now.'

'Of course you do.' The friendly woman saw no harm in her request. 'You'll find his bedroom at the top of the stairs, turn right, and it's the third door along. Mr Caleb's is the one opposite.'

Cat wasn't sure why the other woman added this last piece of information, and she didn't bother to find out either, hurrying from the room.

A knock on the door of Luke's bedroom received no response, and so she knocked again, softly calling his name this time, encouraging him to open the door.

The thing that she had dreaded most happened, the door opposite Luke's flying open, a furious-faced Caleb standing there.

Colour instantly flamed into her cheeks. 'I was looking for Luke——'

'He isn't there,' Caleb rasped coldly, his eyes narrowed.

She drew in a ragged breath. 'I upset him earlier——'

'God, you didn't reject him too, did you?' he rasped scornfully.

'No, of course——'

'Of course not,' he finished icily. 'He's

nineteen and available. Does he look like Harry, too?' he derided.

Cat flinched. 'You know he looks like you——'

'But you don't need a substitute for me,' he bit out. 'I'm all too available to you!' he said with self-disgust.

'Caleb, you don't understand,' she pleaded.

'I understand that you entertained my son while you were in the bath——'

'As he said at the time,' she snapped, 'when I demanded an apology from him for walking in *uninvited*,' she emphasised, 'in his condition he couldn't do much about it.'

'You're an innocent if you don't realise there are—ways,' Caleb bit out.

Cat looked up at him unflinchingly. 'Yes, I am,' she challenged. 'I'm really not that experienced.'

He continued to glare at her, until finally some of the rigidity left his body, and there was pain in his eyes. 'I could have killed you both with my bare hands when I thought you had invited him into your room,' he admitted in a strangulated voice.

'Don't you realise that you——' She broke off with a gasp, her eyes wide.

'I?' Caleb prompted huskily.

She swallowed hard, shaking her head dismissively. 'Caleb, I said some very cruel things to Luke downstairs just now; I have to find him and apologise.'

'He's with his grandfather,' he supplied softly.

'Oh,' she frowned.

'I?' he prompted again, closer now, so close that Cat found herself at eye-level with the dark hair on his chest, his dinner jacket and tie discarded, his shirt partly unbuttoned. 'I, Cat?' he encouraged throatily.

She put her head back to look at him with defiant eyes, 'It was nothing,' she dismissed. 'I'll talk to Luke in the morning.'

'And you'll talk to *me* now,' Caleb held on to her upper arms to prevent her leaving. 'There have been more misunderstandings in this relationship than——'

'We don't have a relationship,' she instantly denied.

'We have a relationship,' he told her gently. 'And it's time for it to progress. Maybe then the misunderstandings will stop. Although I wouldn't count on it,' he said drily.

'Caleb, no,' she protested as he led her inside his bedroom and closed the door.

'Caleb, yes,' he insisted harshly, pulling the combs from her hair so that it cascaded down past her shoulders. 'God! Caleb, *yes!*' He tilted her chin, his thumbtips gently parting her lips for his kiss. 'Just for once admit what you feel for me, Cat,' he encouraged against her mouth. 'Admit it and and take me!'

She wanted him, God, how she wanted him. And not just in her dreams, those ethereal dreams that would no longer come to her. She wanted the flesh and blood man, the man who made her forget everything but him.

She moved the small distance between his mouth and hers, her arms going up about his neck as she kissed him with all the pent-up longing inside her.

'That's it, my darling,' he encouraged throatily. 'Take me.'

He meant it too, giving her no help at all as she undressed him with shaking hands.

'Let me.' He finally took pity on her efforts to unfasten his trousers, his chest already bare, his shirt thrown to the floor. 'You act as if you've never done this before,' he teased, as Cat kept her head bent as she stripped the last of his clothes from him, looking up at him questioningly as he became suddenly still. 'Cat?' He put out a hand and pulled her to her feet, his gaze searching. 'My God—Cat?' He frowned at the innocence he read in her eyes.

'Does it—matter?' Her voice was husky.

'Does it——? My God, Cat, do you have any idea how it makes me feel to know I'll be the first?'

And the last, she silently added. Only this man made her feel this way, and when he no longer wanted her she would be alone again. And she would stay alone.

'Will you give me what you never gave Harry?' he asked in a humbled voice.

Her gaze became troubled. 'Only because he wouldn't take it,' she admitted. 'Caleb, I—I would have——'

'But you didn't,' he smiled. 'You didn't!' he repeated exultantly. 'God, Cat, this is the most beautiful night of my life!'

Tears glistened in her eyes. 'I thought you knew, that you realised——'

'No,' he echoed. 'Otherwise I wouldn't have— I didn't frighten you, did I, those other times I tried to make love to you?' He frowned at the thought.

'I'm a virgin, Caleb, not a simpleton,' she gently mocked.

'And I'm stark naked,' he realised awkwardly, picking his robe up from the chair to pull it on and belt it about his waist. 'Would you like to take a bath? A shower? Or something?' He still frowned.

'I bathed just before dinner, if you remember,' she refused. 'Caleb,' she added softly, '*I'm* supposed to be the shy and innocent one,' she chided. 'You're the man of experience.'

He swallowed hard. 'Never this experience,' he admitted gruffly.

'Luke knew.' She grimaced, as his face darkened ominously. 'He accused me of acting like an outraged virgin when he burst into the bathroom.'

Caleb's scowl deepened. 'That young man needs a lesson in manners around a lady.'

'But not now,' she encouraged throatily.

'No,' he groaned, 'not now.'

Clothes fell to the floor by her hand and Caleb's, she wasn't always sure which, Caleb's lips gentle on her body as she lay naked on the bed beneath him. His kisses on her heated flesh were a torment and a heady delight at the same time, until she cried out at the agony and the ecstasy.

'Patience, my love. Patience,' he softly chided. 'I have no intention of hurting you, no matter how you plead.' He laughed huskily at her groan of outrage, soon making her gasp anew as his lips sought that secret place no other man had known.

Waves of pleasure crashed into themselves as she writhed on the bed, her arms held gently at her sides as she would have pushed Caleb away, the pleasure almost beyond bearing. Almost. Caleb knew exactly how far to take her before stopping the torment, his mouth returning to hers as he languidly caressed her breasts.

'Can I—touch you now?' she asked tentatively, aching to explore the golden beauty of his body.

Pleasure flared in his eyes at her request. 'If you're sure . . .?'

He lay completely still as she made her first tentative caresses, but as she became bolder in her exploration he couldn't hold back the shuddering response of his body to the touch of her hands and lips. Cat felt exultant at his uninhibited response, some inner instinct telling her when it was time to stop.

Caleb lifted her above him, accepting the hard rosebud of her nipple into his mouth as he drank from her. 'You're beautiful, Cat,' he groaned as he rolled over so that she was the one beneath him. 'So very beautiful.' Light butterfly kisses were feathered on her cheeks and brow. 'Do you have any idea how much you please me?' he breathed raggedly, his thighs moving languidly against her in their need.

'As much as you need me, I hope,' she said shyly.

His eyes were liquid fire. 'Now, Cat?' he groaned his need.

'Please,' she urged, her gaze locked with his as he moved above her, gently probing the moistness of her, his eyes darkened with pain at her sharply indrawn breath as he surged completely into her, not moving, just watching as her own pain faded, her eyes becoming wide with the wonder of his possession.

They were no longer two people, but one, joined together where their pleasure was the greatest, giving and taking, and as Caleb's thrusts became harder and quicker Cat knew that she had to give, that she needed to give, that she *did* give, feeling Caleb's body tense before he flowed into her, the two of them still moving gently together even when the crescendo had abated, neither wanting the pleasure to end.

'Oh, Cat,' Caleb groaned as he kissed her languidly. 'Oh God!' He shook uncontrollably.

She held him to her, enjoying the weight of his body, softly caressing his back. 'It was the same for me,' she confided huskily, wonder for the joy they had shared still in her over-bright eyes. 'I never knew there was such—giving.'

He looked down at her with tender eyes. 'Most women would have said pleasure.'

She shook her head. 'It was so much more than that.' Her eyes glowed.

'It was,' he added. 'It still is.'

'Hell just froze over,' she conceded. 'Does it always make you feel this sleepy?' she chattered on, knowing the togetherness he still felt wasn't just the joining of their bodies. She could feel what was happening between them, too, and she needed time to accept what she already thought she felt for this man. With Harry she had never needed to question the rightness of their love; with Caleb there was so much to question,

whether it *was* love being one of the things she
needed to know.

He laughed indulgently, taking her with him as
he rolled on to his side, their bodies still joined.
'No,' he chuckled as she blinked like a sleepy
feline. 'But I can see that tonight I'll have to
allow you to go to sleep.'

Her eyes widened. 'You mean you aren't
tired?'

The returning hardness of his body was answer
enough, and he laughed softly as she blushed.
'Only a little,' he drawled.

'Not even a little,' she gasped at the involuntary
movements of his body inside her, wide awake
again herself now. 'Caleb, can we—are you——?'

'God, yes,' he groaned. 'I could go on making
love to you all night!'

And he did, in every way there was, whether he
be tormenting her with slow caresses that made
her beg, or fiercely taking her with hard thrusts
of his body. There was no question of a giver or a
taker in their heated lovemaking, they both gave,
until, for now, they were too exhausted to give
any more.

Caleb's arms reached out for her instinctively
as she slid from his side the next morning, but
she managed to reassure his sleepy movements
with a lingering kiss on the mouth, leaving the
bedroom as quietly as she could, breathing a sigh
of relief when she reached her own bedroom
without running into any of the Steele staff.

Although perhaps that wasn't so surprising; it
was only six-thirty in the morning!

She loved Caleb Steele. This morning there

was no doubt in her mind about how she felt. She couldn't have given herself the way that she had, have Caleb give himself to her in the same way, if she hadn't already been in love with him.

What happened now?

What did she want to happen?

She wanted Caleb to love her as she loved him!

Why was that so important? She surely wasn't expecting him to marry her?

She was right to scorn that possibility. Caleb had been a single man since he was her age, had enjoyed his bachelor status to the full, had no reason to settle on one woman and marry her.

But she wanted to marry him! Once again she knew the feeling of loving a man completely, of wanting to be with him, during good times and bad, of wanting to give him children. Any child that Caleb fathered would have to have those dark blue or black eyes of the Steele family, but if they inherited her blonde colouring they would be beautiful children.

But last night Caleb had only wanted to evict the ghost from her life, and while she knew her love for Harry would always be a part of her she knew it was no longer her whole life, that last night Caleb had become the centre of all her hopes and dreams for the future, the future she had believed died with Harry. Would Caleb want that? She didn't think so.

She returned sadly to her original question; what happened now?

It was a question to which she had found no answer by the time she joined Lucien Steele for breakfast in his suite, at his request, not having seen Caleb since she kissed him good morning two hours ago.

Black eyes studied her intently, and Cat felt herself blush self-consciously. Lucien no longer even needed to try and read her dreams in her eyes, the vividness of her time in Caleb's arms last night was glowing in them!

'Miss Howard,' he drawled, standing up with a politeness that was belied by the searching intensity of his gaze. 'Or may I call you Cat?' he added softly.

'Now that you're my son's lover,' Cat felt as if he had said. 'Please,' she invited distantly. 'This is a beautiful suite,' she added, to fill the awkwardness, genuinely liking the warm comfort of the rooms Lucien Steele had made into his home the last two years.

'Thank you,' he accepted drily. 'You're a very beautiful young woman.'

She blushed anew at his bluntness. 'I—thank you,' she accepted uncomfortably.

He smiled. 'I'm not the first member of my family to tell you so,' he mocked.

'Mr Steele——'

'Lucien,' he put in softly. 'Which of them told you you're beautiful, Caleb or Luke?' he mused as if greatly enjoying himself.

'Both of them—I think,' she frowned. 'I——'

'Really?' he chuckled softly. 'I trust you ignored my grandson?'

'Concerning that, yes,' she nodded. 'Otherwise he's a little difficult to ignore.'

Lucien sobered. 'You made quite an impression on him, too!'

She felt a sinking feeling in the pit of her stomach. 'If it's about last night——'

'Which part of it?' he prompted in amusement.

'Mr Steele——'

'Caleb told me you have an annoying habit of becoming formal when you're embarrassed or angry,' he spoke conversationally. 'Which one are you now?'

'Both!' she snapped.

'I can see that you are,' he sympathised regretfully. 'It was wrong of me to tease you in that way. Let's sit down and have breakfast, and I'll tell you all about my marriage to Sonia.'

For a moment she continued to glare at him suspiciously, feeling a little like a fish must feel when it's being wound in on the line, unsure whether it would become the next meal or be put back in the water. But if he wanted to play word-games, let him. She didn't have anything to be ashamed of.

'I would prefer it if you didn't sit and take notes while we eat.' Lucien accepted the coffee she poured for him. 'Anything you don't remember we can go over again another time.'

She listened in fascination as he began to talk of that life in Hollywood during the forties that had never been reproduced: the parties, the cars, the scandals, and interwoven through it all his ten years of marriage to Sonia Harrison.

'She was truly a "star" in the fullest sense of the word.' His eyes glowed as he remembered his wife's beauty. 'I was happy just to live in her shadow.'

'Oh, but——'

'I was a famous man in my own right,' he softly finished for her. 'Not like Sonia. She was *the* star of the time. I was called Mr Harrison by hotel porters, in restaurants, by fans we met in the street, even by some of the actors themselves.'

'Didn't you mind?' Cat frowned, able to imagine how awkward that must have been for him.

'God, no,' he dismissed without rancour. 'I would have *become* Mr Harrison just to remain at her side as her husband.'

Cat had never seen so much love and pride shown in anyone's face as she saw in Lucien Steele's at that moment. It was obvious that he had adored his wife. That he still did.

Suddenly he frowned at Cat. 'Have you ever seen any of her films?'

She nodded. 'She was very beautiful.'

'Mesmerising,' he breathed softly. 'Everyone loved her. And she loved—only me. And our child. She loved Caleb from the moment he was born. I began to hope that night that she——'

'Yes?' she prompted as he broke off.

His eyes were dark now, the love fading from them. 'A star has many facets, Cat,' he told her slowly. 'Each as bright—and unyielding, as the last.'

Cat sat tensely in her chair, waiting for him to continue as he seemed to have lapsed off into some memory she had no right to. He drew himself back from the hell he had receded to with effort, looking at her with pain-glazed eyes.

'Jealousy is the most destructive emotion there is,' he stated flatly.

She could understand how he could feel the emotion when his wife was constantly with handsome movie stars, men who often felt they had to make a conquest, whether the woman was married or not. It couldn't have been easy being the husband of a screen goddess.

Lucien's mouth twisted as he studied her. 'I can see what you're thinking,' he drawled. 'And you're completely wrong in your conclusions,' he sighed. 'I wasn't the one that was jealous.'

She frowned her confusion. 'Your wife . . .?' She suddenly realised what he meant, dumbfounded by the claim when this man had obviously adored the woman.

'Yes.' His sigh was heavier this time. 'Of course there was no reason for the jealousy,' he stated unnecessarily. 'I worshipped the ground Sonia glided across. But jealousy can't be reasoned with. And it can't be ignored either.'

Cat sat stiffly as she waited for him to go on, sure that in a moment she was going to hear something she would rather not know—and completely unable to stop it from happening!

'There were arguments, fights,' he revealed harshly. 'Savage fights,' he added in a sickened voice. 'When Sonia seemed to lose all reason, would throw things, anything she could get her hands on.'

Cat didn't want to hear any more of this, it was too personal, too intimate. 'Mr Steele——'

His eyes blazed with anger at her interruption. 'You came here to hear about my marriage to Sonia, Cat, so stop being embarrassed and listen!' he grated. 'Sit down,' he ordered as she stood up.

'Just because this isn't the pretty fairy story you wanted is no reason for you to run away from it.'

'I'm not running away!'

'Then sit down!'

She sat. 'Please, go on,' she invited shakily, feeling as if she were an eavesdropper on intimacies that were no one's concern but this man's. And yet she knew that wasn't strictly true, knew that the picture of Sonia Harrison that her husband was describing in no way matched the press releases of the time where she was known for her beauty and sweet-temperedness.

'I intended to,' he bit out coldly. 'Sonia was a human being, with all the frailties that go along with that; she wasn't the plaster screen goddess they tried to make of her. Maybe if they hadn't tried to mould her in that way she wouldn't have hit out with those angry scenes,' he shrugged. 'The only thing that recompensed for them was the tempestuous making up afterwards,' he sighed. 'Except one night we didn't get as far as making up, the night she threw one thing too many.' He flinched at the memory. 'An oil lamp,' he revealed flatly, as Cat looked puzzled.

She gasped, frowning her disbelief of what he was implying, the steadiness of his gaze showing her that every word he spoke was the truth. 'The night of the fire . . .?' she realised.

He closed his eyes to shut out the pain of that memory. 'Yes,' he breathed. 'The place went up like a tinder-box. Caleb managed to climb out of a window in his bedroom, but I couldn't find Sonia after the first flames went up.'

This was the 'wandering' Caleb had warned

her about and feared his father doing, the 'unpleasant things he said that didn't make sense'. But they did make sense, shockingly so. All the news reports at the time had said the fire had started accidentally, but it hadn't; Sonia Harrison had started that fire, if not deliberately, then in a burst of uncontrollable anger, anger none of the public believed her to be capable of.

She moistened her lips. 'Why are you telling me all this?' she encouraged softly.

'Because I'm tired,' he told her heavily. 'And for another reason I think you guessed the first time you looked at me.'

He was dying.

CHAPTER NINE

'YES,' he smiled sadly as he saw the realisation in her eyes. 'At least Sonia didn't know she was going to die that night. She wouldn't have thrown the lamp if she had,' he said wryly. 'Sonia loved to be alive.'

'Can't anything be done? For you, I mean,' Cat frowned.

'No, my dear,' He gave her an encouraging smile. 'And I'm not sure I would have wanted it if it could,' he admitted gruffly.

'Oh but——'

'Cat,' he cut in firmly. 'I'm not afraid to die; I've lived for seventy-four years, too many of them without Sonia.'

Seventy-four wasn't old, not in this day and age. 'Surely Caleb——'

'He's called in all the specialists,' Lucien assured her softly. 'To no avail. But it doesn't really matter, because I'll be glad it's all going to end at last. I wanted to die when Sonia did, but it wasn't to be, and I had the responsibility of our son to think of. What's your excuse?' he asked suddenly.

Cat blinked. 'I beg your pardon?'

'I know you loved your young man,' he sympathised gently. 'But it wasn't enough to join him.'

She swallowed hard. 'What do you mean?'

'When Luke asked you last night how you had

survived after your fiancé was killed on your wedding day you said you had no choice, that you hadn't been in the car with him.' Lucien watched her with narrowed eyes.

'He told you—all that?' she gasped.

'Caleb treats you as he has no other woman; I had to know the reason for that.'

'And you think it's because I lost Harry in that way?' she demanded to know.

'No,' he denied drily. 'Although it does explain a few things. Cat, don't you realise you did have a choice the day your young man died; you had the choice whether to go on without him or to join him.'

'Suicide?' she choked. 'How can you say that when you—when you——'

'I told you, I had our child to think about. I couldn't deny him both of his parents. Who did you have?' he prompted.

'Myself,' she burst out without thinking. 'I didn't want to die. I didn't want to die . . .' She was crying as she realised what she was saying, her face buried in her hands.

'Of course you didn't, my dear.' Lucien's hand squeezed her arm understandingly. 'Who would my Caleb have loved if you had?' he gently rebuked.

She shook her head. 'Caleb doesn't love me.'

'Doesn't he?' his father mused. 'Well, we shall see. I'm sorry I was so cruel just now, Cat—I'm sure Caleb wouldn't have allowed it if he had known; he doesn't like anyone to be cruel to his little cat,' he said drily. 'I only wanted to show you that although you loved your young man you chose to live after he had gone, and now you have

to be strong enough to move on, to make the life
for yourself that's open to you, and not to live
with the memories that are really no life at all.'

'You have,' she accused.

'Tell me, Cat, how would you feel if Caleb
were to die tomorrow?'

All the colour drained from her face, her eyes
deep green pools of pain.

'How, Cat?' Lucien prompted roughly.

Her lips moved stiffly, almost of their own
volition. 'I don't know.' Her voice came out in a
strangulated rasp. But she did know, she *did*! And
it was a betrayal.

'You didn't love Harry any less than you love
Caleb,' Lucien assured her at her tragic look.
'Just in a different way. If he had lived, your love
for him would have grown deeper, more intense,
the way that you now love Caleb.'

'I'm not even sure I do love Caleb.' Again she
spoke with less than honesty, and she knew that
she wasn't fooling Lucien Steele either.

'You're sure, Cat,' he chided. 'You just aren't
willing to admit it yet. Why do you think I told
you about Sonia and myself if not to show you
the futility of wasting your life in regrets.'

Cat frowned. 'But you've never remarried.'

'Because Sonia was that deeper more intense
love as well as my youthful love,' he explained
gently. 'I realise you need time to take in all that
I've said, but I think you already know and
understand what I've been trying to say to you.'

She did, of course she did. She had more or
less grown up with Harry, and their falling in
love had happened so naturally they had had no

doubts about their future together, confident they would grow and continue to love together. And they would have done if Harry hadn't died. But he *had* been taken from her, and she had continued to grow on her own. So that she could fall in love with Caleb.

Lucien squeezed her arm again. 'And now I'd like to thank you for helping Luke the way you have,' he said briskly.

'Helping him?' she repeated dazedly.

'He's been a hell-raiser since they diagnosed my weakened heart two years ago, but last night you helped him to accept my death. He suddenly realised, after hearing of the death of a nineteen-year-old man who had everything to live for, what I've tried to tell him so many times, that I'm seventy-four years old. You made him realise that isn't such a bad age to die, not when you've had as much out of life as I have.'

That reckless light she had seen in Luke's eyes, that affinity she had briefly felt with him. She hadn't guessed it was because of anything like this!

'Luke has been blaming the whole world for my illness, I'm afraid,' Lucien sighed sadly. 'Including Caleb.'

It explained so much: Luke's disrespect for his father, his bouts of temper, his viciousness, his outright cruelty on occasion. She had seen all that in Luke's face that day, just as yesterday she had seen death in this man's face, she just hadn't put the two facts together.

'I had no idea . . .' she groaned. 'I tried to find him last night to apologise——'

'Any apologies that need to be made should come from him,' his grandfather rasped. 'He's acted disgracefully where you're concerned.'

'I didn't understand.' She shook her head.

'There's no excuse for what he did to you,' Lucien insisted sternly. 'It could have turned out so much worse than it has.'

'Even so——'

'Even so nothing, my dear,' he cut in firmly. 'I told him exactly what I thought of his actions when he came to see me last night. Hopefully he's come to his senses now.'

She certainly hoped so, no matter how it had been achieved. The self-destructive course Luke had been on could only have ended one way if he wasn't stopped, as it almost had when he had driven off the bridge and only succeeded in breaking his leg.

'As to what you do about the things I've told you about Sonia and I, I leave that entirely up to you,' Lucien dismissed.

'You want me to print it? About the fire, everything?' Her eyes were wide.

His gaze was steady. 'I want you to do what you think best.'

'But——'

'Whatever you think best, Cat,' he repeated firmly.

She swallowed hard, knowing she couldn't possibly make public his confidences, that it was too personal and private to this man and his family. 'Lucien, I—what is it?' She suddenly realised he had become very pale, almost grey. 'Mr Steele?' she said sharply, moving across the short distance that separated them, clasping his hands as they lay limply against his leg, shocked at how cold they were considering the warmth in the room.

'I'm—sorry—you—had to—see this,' he choked.

'Oh dear God ...!' She looked about her frantically as she realised what was happening, knowing she had to get help for him but frightened of leaving him alone like this.

'Get—Caleb,' he managed to gasp between stiff lips. 'He knows—what to do.'

'But you——'

'Get him, Cat,' he choked. 'And please try to include Luke—in your—love for my son. They're going to—need you.'

'Lucien, no——'

'Please—get—Caleb,' he gasped again.

She ran from the suite and down the corridor to Caleb's room. He had just finished dressing, his eyes darkening warmly as she burst into the room.

'Good morning, sweetheart.' His voice was huskily indulgent. 'You should have woken me——'

'Caleb, it's your father,' she cut in forcefully, his lazy expression turning to one of watchful intensity. 'We were talking when suddenly he— Caleb, you have to go to him!' Her panic increased. 'He just collapsed.'

He pushed past her out of the room, running down the corridor to rush through the door that Cat had left open in her rush to find assistance.

Cat followed, watching as he examined his

father as he still sat in the chair, his cheeks
appearing hollow now, his eyes seeming to have
sunk into his head as he looked at his son.

Cat had never felt so helpless in her life,
standing numbly just inside the doorway, looking
dully at Norm as he appeared behind her.

'I heard shouting,' he explained, quickly taking
in the scene across the room. 'Caleb——'

His employer turned to him with fierce eyes as
he tried to make his father more comfortable.
'Get her out of here,' he bit out tautly.

'But——'

'Just get her out, Norm,' he instructed
savagely. 'And then call the doctor and find
Luke. At this time of morning the latter
shouldn't be too difficult!' he rasped.

Cat looked at him searchingly, before she was
led away by Norm. She wasn't looking for love,
certainly not that warm desire of a short time ago,
but surely there should have been some sort of
understanding pass between them, a searching
and giving of the compassion she so longed to
give him. Caleb had just coldly turned away.

She leant into Norm's side as he led her back
to her bedroom, wanting to be with Caleb during
this anxious time, but knowing he had rejected
any feeling of closeness they might have had
when he had ordered Norm to take her away
from him. Lucien had been wrong, Caleb didn't
love her, he couldn't if he wouldn't let her be at
his side now, when he needed someone so badly.

The doctor arrived a short time later. Cat
heard his car in the driveway and went to the
window to watch him enter the house. She had

little else to do but watch the comings and goings to the house during the morning, no one feeling the need to come and tell her what was happening, or how Lucien was.

She refused Mrs McDonald's offer of lunch, the older woman telling her that the doctor was coming back later to see Lucien, that Caleb and Luke were sitting with him.

Norman Bruce came to her room shortly after the other woman had left.

He looked strained, older somehow, although Cat couldn't quite have said in what way. 'Do you have your case packed?' he enquired briskly.

Her eyes widened. 'Why, yes. But—how's Lucien?' she frowned.

'Holding his own,' he bit out tersely. 'The car is waiting for us outside, if you're ready to go.'

The arrangement had been for her to leave after lunch on Sunday, and she had packed her case before dinner last night with that in mind, but after Lucien's collapse she hadn't given it another thought. 'You can't mean me to leave now?' she protested.

'Why not?'

'Lucien!' she reminded him in an exasperated voice.

'Cat,' Norm spoke gently now. 'It's Caleb's orders that you go. Now.'

She felt as if he had struck her in the chest, physically knocked all the breath from her body, leaving her weak and aching with a pain that wasn't in the least physical. 'Why?' she choked.

Norm shrugged. 'He just told me to take you back to London. I'm not paid to ask why, Cat.'

He sighed at the distress she couldn't hide. 'Honey, it's best that you leave,' he encouraged gently.

It wasn't best for her, so it had to be best for Caleb. He didn't want her in his home or his life. 'I'm ready.' She stood up numbly.

Norm gave her a searching look, seeming to wish there were something he could say to comfort her, and finding there was nothing he could say.

They both maintained their own troubled silence as they left the house, during the drive to the airport, and on the flight back to London, Cat having no interest this time in the brightly lit city in dusk's early glow.

'Thank you.' She stopped inside the airport, looking up at Norm with pained eyes.

'Caleb told me to take you all the way home,' he told her ruefully.

'I don't give a damn——' She broke off, her eyes flashing deeply green, the fire fading from their depths as she saw the unshakable determination in his face. 'I can easily get a taxi from here,' she informed him dully.

'There's a car waiting for us outside.' He kept a firm hold of her case as he strode purposefully towards the exit.

Cat almost had to run to keep up with him, keeping her face averted once they were in the car so that he shouldn't see just how upset she was, having difficulty holding back the tears now.

'Cat.' Norm finally touched her hand, holding on to it as she would have flinched away.

'Have you done this sort of thing before?'

She turned on him angrily, pulling her hand away.

He frowned. 'What sort of thing?'

She swallowed down her shame at the accusation she had been about to make. Of course he didn't usually escort the women from Caleb's life, there had been extenuating circumstances. And she doubted if normally she would have been put out of Caleb's life quite this abruptly; he just had no use for her during his father's illness.

'It doesn't matter.' She shook her head. 'Please convey how sorry I am about Lucien to—to the family,' she amended gruffly.

'I'll do that.' He squeezed her hand. 'And I'm sure Caleb will be in touch as soon as he can.'

'Did he say that?' she pounced eagerly.

'Well—no. But——'

The hope faded from her eyes, and she turned away to see the car was stopping outside the house she and Vikki shared. 'Thanks for bringing me home,' she told Norm brightly. 'I suppose you'll be returning to Scotland now?'

'Yes,' he acknowledged softly.

'I'm sorry you were given this task,' she sighed. 'I'm sure the last thing you wanted to do was leave there now to bring me home.'

'I'll let you know when—what happens,' he amended huskily.

'I'd like it if you could,' she nodded, getting out of the car.

She didn't wait outside to watch the car leave, walking into the house as if in a dream, barely aware of the voices in the lounge, although she assumed it was Vikki and Sam. Dropping her suitcase down on her bed she sat down beside it, burying her face in her hands as she wept. She wept for Lucien, although she knew he spoke the truth when he said he would be relieved when he was finally granted release to join Sonia. And she cried for Caleb, the man whom she loved more than anything and anyone in the world. She even cried for Luke, and she hoped that he and Caleb would finally find each other in their shared worry over Lucien.

'I thought I heard—hey,' Vikki's pleasure turned to concern as she saw how upset Cat was. 'What's happened?' She came down on her haunches beside the bed.

Cat couldn't hold back any more, everything tumbling out, the whole traumatic weekend.

'He's just worried about his father,' Vikki sooothed when she heard of the way Caleb had ordered her departure.

She shook her head. 'I tried to tell myself that,' she choked. 'But it was more than that, he just didn't want me there.'

'I'm sure you're wrong——'

'Then why am I here and he's there coping with this alone?' she demanded shakily.

Vikki chewed on her bottom lip. 'Look.' She straightened. 'I don't know all the details of last night—and I don't want to,' she added hastily as Cat blushed. 'But I do think you're over-reacting because you're tired and upset. I'm going to get you a nice cup of tea, and after you've drunk it you're going to have a nap——'

'I couldn't sleep,' she gasped.

'A cup of tea and then some rest,' Vikki insisted firmly. 'I'll listen out for the telephone, just in case this Norm calls,' she added gently.

Cat obediently drank the tea Vikki brought her, sure she wouldn't be able to sleep as she lay down on the bed. But her exhausted body had other ideas about that, and it was the ringing of the telephone that finally woke her. She woke with a start at the first ring, hearing Vikki pick up the receiver downstairs before she rang through to the extension in the bedroom.

'For you, Cat,' she told her gently before putting the call through.

Cat moistened suddenly dry lips. 'Norm?'

'Luke,' his youthful voice instantly corrected.

She swallowed hard; he was the last person she had been expecting. 'Is—has——?'

'He's gone, Cat,' he said gruffly. 'Quite peacefully in the end. I—I thought you would like to know. Norm said you had asked him to call, and I—well, I'm not very good at apologising, but——'

'Please,' she cut in shakily. 'It isn't necessary,' she dismissed. 'I—I'm so sorry about your grandfather.' She may have only known him a short time but she had grown fond of the elderly man.

'Yes,' he acknowledged sadly.

The shock of Luke being the one to telephone her, after waking so suddenly, had thrown her completely off-guard, and she had trouble thinking straight. 'I'm sure it's too soon for you to know when it will be, but I—I'd like to come to the funeral. If no one would mind,' she added hesitantly.

'The funeral is tentatively arranged for Friday. It's going to be up here because Granpop loved the place so much.' He paused. 'And, I'm afraid—it's for family only.'

He really sounded as if he genuinely hated to rebuff her, and Cat didn't need to ask who had made that decision. 'I understand,' she accepted abruptly. 'And I really am sorry about your grandfather.'

'Yes.'

'Thank you for letting me know, I'm sure there are a lot of other things you have to do.'

'None quite as important,' he told her with sincerity.

'If there's anything I can do—of course there isn't,' she dismissed awkwardly.

'Cat, for what it's worth I think Dad is wrong to shut you out like this,' he rasped. 'I tried to reason with him, but he's adamant.'

'It's all right,' she assured him firmly, the pain in her chest ten times worse than it had been earlier. 'I'll send some flowers instead. If that's all right?' she asked anxiously. Surely Caleb couldn't object to that?

'Of course,' Luke assured her softly. 'He liked pansies. He always said they reminded him of grandmother's eyes,' he recalled emotionally. 'Look, I'd better go now, Cat.' He fought to retain control until the call had finished. 'I just wanted to be the one to let you know.'

She thanked him once again before ringing off.

Caleb. She had taken him, as he had asked her to do, and he had rejected her and the love that could have shared his pain at the loss of his father.

CHAPTER TEN

THE saying 'life goes on' appeared to be a true one; life did indeed go on, but for Cat it had never been so grey. The day of the funeral arrived and she sent her flowers, the pansies Luke had suggested, and her heart cried out to be with Caleb at a time when he needed those that loved him by his side.

She had heard nothing from him, hadn't really expected to, knew that he had to be very busy after his father's sudden death, knowing he had probably forgotten her existence in the trauma of the last few days. From the many reports on television and in the newspapers about the family, they had known no peace.

Maybe it was selfish to dwell on her own unhappiness in the circumstances, but she knew Lucien had wanted her to be with Caleb, and she missed and loved Caleb more than she had ever thought she could care for a man again, hadn't been able to stop the love she felt for him from blossoming and growing until it filled her whole life. Losing Harry had been horrific, but at least she had had the comfort of knowing he loved her as she loved him; what she felt for Caleb was soul-destroying in its futility.

For years she had been afraid to love again in case she lost that second love as she had the first, but she was finding that to love Caleb and not

have that love returned was worse than losing
Harry the way that she had. If Lucien were here
to ask her again, 'how would you feel if Caleb
died tomorrow?' she wouldn't hesitate to answer
him truthfully this time; Caleb may not be dead,
but he was as far removed from her as if he were,
and she felt like dying herself!

The news report of the funeral that evening did
nothing to dispel those feelings of despair,
Deanna Trent clinging daintily to Caleb's arm at
the graveside, the beauty of her face half-revealed
by the black lace veil of her hat. She looked
delicate and tragic, and she was obviously still
considered very much a part of the 'family only'
Luke had mentioned.

Caleb looked grim, older by ten years as he
held the grief-stricken Luke to his side, his
arm about his son's shoulders.

Cat felt as if she intruded upon a very private
moment, getting up to switch off the television
set, restlessly pacing the room.

'I've got to get out,' she finally decided. 'I've
got to go and see Susan some time this weekend,
so I might as well go over now. And then
tomorrow I could arrange to go down to my
parents for the weekend.'

Vikki frowned as Cat pulled on her jacket. 'I'm
sure the fact that his ex-wife was at the funeral
didn't mean a thing,' she consoled gently. 'She
hasn't been married to number five all that long!'

'Deanna Trent has nothing to do with my
wanting to go out,' she defended.

'Doesn't she?' Vikki sighed as Cat's expression
remained stubborn. 'Love, the man's had a

frantic week. I'm sure he'll come and see you once everything has settled down a little.'

'No, he won't,' she denied dully. 'People are usually drawn together by tragedy, not pulled apart. It's over,' she added briskly. 'And now I have to pick up the pieces and get on with my life.'

'Again.'

She looked sharply at her friend. 'What do you mean?'

'Cat, you may not be able to do it a second time. Losing Harry almost killed you; I'm afraid for you this time,' Vikki admitted with blunt honesty.

'There's no need,' she shook her head. 'I'll survive.'

'Will you?'

'Yes!' She would survive because she had to, because she had no choice. Life didn't just end because it was willed to do so. And she knew that before her pain was over she would will it many times, as Lucien had because of Sonia.

Once she got out of the house she knew she didn't feel up to going to her sister's, to putting a brave face on everything, to being part of that happy family unit that belonged to Sue, Daniel and Josh. And so she walked, everywhere and nowhere it seemed, oblivious to the biting wind ripping into her.

Where was Caleb now? Was his ex-wife with him? Were Luke and his parents sharing a quiet family dinner together somewhere?

Oh God, the torment of not knowing was like nothing else she had ever known! She was jealous just at the thought of Caleb being with another woman when she so desperately wanted to be with him herself. It must have been obvious the night she had spent in his arms that she was falling in love with him, and she had thought, had hoped, that he felt the same way.

'Where have you been?' Vikki demanded as soon as she entered the house.

'I——'

'And don't tell me you've been to Susan's because I called there,' Vikki accused, impatiently helping Cat off with her coat before hanging it up.

'I went for a walk instead.' She frowned at Vikki's unwarranted aggression.

'I've been going frantic!'

'I'm sorry,' she said dazedly. 'I didn't mean to worry you.'

'Well you did,' her friend snapped.

'Why?' She shook her head in puzzlement.

'It's about ten degrees below out there, you didn't go to your sister's as you said you were going to, and you ask why I was worried about you!' Vikki glared.

'I didn't notice the cold, and I didn't feel like going to Sue's once I got out,' she explained patiently. 'And now I think I'll go to bed——'

'You can't do that!' Vikki protested, pulling at her arm. 'His smile isn't as cold tonight, his expression isn't quite as remote, but I've still bored him out of his mind trying to make polite conversation!' she told Cat forcefully.

All the colour drained from her face. 'Caleb . . .?' she managed to gasp. 'He's here?'

Vikki nodded quickly. 'In the lounge. And, Cat, he looks awful,' she groaned. 'Much worse than on the television earlier.'

Caleb was here. Not somewhere private with Deanna, but here in her home, waiting for *her*. Nothing else was important. 'I'll go to him.' A glow began in her eyes, although she was aware that his visit here tonight could mean nothing. But it could also mean everything, and that was what she was hoping for!

'Cat,' Vikki touched her arm. 'Good luck.'

'Thank you,' she smiled tremulously.

'No matter when he leaves—*if* he leaves,' Vikki amended ruefully, 'I want you to come and tell me what happened!'

She nodded, taking a deep controlling breath before entering the lounge. Vikki was right, Caleb did look awful, those beautiful dark eyes full of shadows, deep lines etched into his face. He looked thinner, too, and so utterly weary.

He stood up as she closed the door behind her to lean back against it, the dark suit he had worn earlier in the day replaced by an open-necked blue shirt and tailored blue trousers.

She had had only her memories of him since her time with him in Scotland, not even her dreams returning, and she drank in the sight of him, wishing she could lay in his arms now and banish the unhappiness from his face and heart.

But she didn't move, couldn't move.

'How have you been?' he asked gruffly.

She moistened her suddenly stiff lips. 'Fine,' she nodded abruptly. 'Er—how's Luke?'

'Very well. He sent his regards.'

'Really?' she frowned. 'That was nice of him.'

Caleb's mouth twisted. 'Wasn't it?' he drawled.

'I—er—I was sorry about your father,' she told him awkwardly.

He nodded abruptly. 'Your flowers arrived today. Thank you.'

How could two people who had made love together act like stilted strangers? It didn't make sense, and yet Cat knew she was as guilty of it as Caleb was.

'How's Norm?' she asked politely.

'Coping,' he derided.

'And—and your wife?' She kept her expression deliberately bland.

His eyes narrowed. 'You saw her?'

'On the television earlier,' Cat nodded.

He gave a deep sigh. 'Deanna is the same as she always was, beautifully made up for the cameras! She liked my father no more than he liked her, but for Luke's sake I couldn't make a scene about her being there today.'

'I see,' Cat nodded.

Caleb frowned. 'Her being there had nothing to do with me,' he rasped.

'It's really none of my concern even if it did,' she pointed out gently. 'I—I was just a little surprised to see her there, that's all,' she dismissed lightly.

'So was I,' he admitted ruefully. 'But I didn't come here to talk about Deanna or Luke, and certainly not my father's funeral,' he frowned. 'I stayed away as long as I could, Cat, but I need you so much.'

'Need—me?' she repeated dazedly. 'How can

you say that when——' She broke off, chewing on her bottom lip, knowing Caleb had gone through enough this last week without her hurling recriminations at him.

'When?' he prompted softly.

'It doesn't matter,' she shook her head, avoiding his gaze.

'Yes,' he insisted huskily. 'Yes, I have a feeling it matters very much.' He took her in his arms, moulding the length of her body to his. 'Cat, you have to realise how much I need you,' he insisted urgently.

She looked at him with pained eyes. 'How can you say that when you pushed me away like you did?' she said, voicing the reason for that pain.

'When?' he encouraged softly.

'When your father—God, I'm so sorry he died.' Her mouth trembled emotionally. 'I liked him.'

'He liked you, too. And he approved of you as the woman I love.'

'You don't love me,' she denied. 'You can't.'

'Only a fool would say that, Cat,' he gently chided. 'And you're far from being that.'

'Thank you!'

He smiled. 'God, I've missed you and the way you can make me laugh,' he groaned. 'The last week has been—bleak,' he grimaced.

Her expression softened at the weary look to his face. 'Caleb, I love you.'

'I know,' he told her gently.

Indignation flared in her eyes. 'I only knew it myself the night we made love.'

'Did you?' he mused. 'That was the night I realised it, too.'

'How?' she demanded.

His smile was gentle now. 'Because of the way you were with me. Cat, no woman had ever given herself to me the way you did that night. I realise I shouldn't mention those other women now, but it's because of them that I knew how different it was with you. I wanted you physically from the start, but I also want to protect you, watch you grow round with my children, to love those children, grow old with you.'

Cat drew away from him. 'All that is sharing,' she said slowly.

He frowned at her withdrawal. 'Yes.'

'Just the good things, Caleb?' she rasped.

'I don't understand,' he shook his head.

Perhaps not, but she suddenly did, had realised what he had done as soon as he said he wanted to protect her. 'What about the painful things in life, Caleb? Or is that what you intend protecting me from?' she prompted softly.

'If I can,' he acknowledged harshly.

'That was why you sent me away on Sunday, wasn't it?' she sighed. 'Caleb?' she prompted again.

He swung away from her. 'You've already been through enough,' he rasped. 'I couldn't ask you to go through my father's death with me. I wouldn't have taken you anywhere near him if I'd thought it could have happened while you were there.' His eyes were pained. 'Not after Harry.'

'Caleb.' Cat moved to stand against him, her arms about his waist as her head rested on his rapidly rising and falling chest. 'Darling, I love you, and your pain is my pain, even the pain of losing someone you loved.' She looked up at him. 'I so much wanted to be with you then.'

'My father said you would feel that way—yes, he was able to talk a little before he died,' Caleb said softly at her surprised look. 'He told me you were strong enough to be at my side.'

'Then you also know that I know——'

'About my mother?' He nodded.

'Do you know why he told me about that?' She looked at him anxiously.

He nodded. 'Do you?'

'Because of Harry,' she acknowledged. 'Because after what Luke had told him about Harry he wanted me to realise that I had chosen to live after Harry died, that I had fallen in love with you and now had a responsibility to that love.'

'Did it work?'

'You know it did.' She smiled at him tremulously. 'Although I was already half-way to acknowledging that fact without any prompting from anyone.'

'Dad just wanted to make sure you got the final push in the right direction,' Caleb said drily.

'By telling me about your mother,' she sighed. 'I can't ever write about that, you know,' she groaned. 'It's too personal.'

'Dad knew that,' he smiled.

'He did?' Her eyes were wide.

'Of course,' he drawled. 'He knew you were in love with me, and he knew I was in love with you. He took a risk on the newest member of the Steele family not wanting to betray his secret.'

'But I—Steele family?' she repeated gruffly.

'I'm trying to ask you to marry me, Cat,' he grimaced. 'But I'm not doing a very good job of it,' he acknowledged drily. 'I don't have my father's gift with words, or Luke's brashness in going after what he wants, and I seem to have made a complete hash of protecting the only woman I've ever loved——'

'When she didn't need protecting,' Cat told him sternly, love shining in her eyes.

'When she didn't need protecting,' he conceded huskily. 'But I do love you, so much, and I would very much like you to be my wife.'

'Like?'

He grinned. 'I told you I don't have a way with words. But, I might add, you aren't too forthcoming yourself.'

'Sorry?' she frowned.

'With words. One little one to be precise,' he encouraged softly. 'And please make it a yes!' he groaned his need of her.

Her expression was one of extreme tenderness. 'You know it's yes. I love you, I want to grow round with your children, to love those children, to grow old with you. But most of all I want to share everything with you, the sadness as well as the happiness. Maybe when I met you I was avoiding all emotional involvement,' she conceded. 'Believed that if I didn't get involved again I couldn't be hurt. But falling in love with you changed all that, made me feel alive in a way I never want to end.'

'I should have known you would feel like this,' he groaned, holding her in his arms. 'You're too real yourself to accept anything but reality, even if it is a painful one. I'm sorry if I misjudged the situation with my father. I needed you so damned much today!'

She gently touched his cheek. 'I love you even more for trying to shield me from that,' she assured him. 'But I won't break.'

'I know that now.' He spoke into her hair as he held her to him. 'When will you marry me?'

'As soon as it can be arranged,' she said without hesitation. 'But how do you think Luke will react to us wanting to get married?' She frowned her uncertainty. 'I seem to remember he wasn't too happy at the idea of having a stepmother at his age, and I don't want to be the cause of any more friction between you.'

'Luke and I have talked out a lot of things the last week. It's going to take him a while to get over his grandfather's death, but he will get over it. He knows how I feel about you, and I'm sure he won't cause any friction. He——' Caleb broke off, frowning down at Cat as she began to chuckle. 'What's so funny?' he asked quizzically.

'Luke's face when I begin to "grow round" with your baby,' she giggled. 'It should be a sight worth seeing. If he thinks he's too old for a stepmother wait until we present him with a baby brother or sister!'

Caleb's eyes gleamed his own amusement. 'Catherine Howard, soon-to-be-Steele, I think you've developed a vindictive sense of humour.'

'Wicked, isn't it?' she grinned.

Caleb sobered, his eyes devouring her. 'God, I'm glad Luke put you in my bed that night,' he said intensely. 'I don't think I could live without you.'

She knew she had only begun to live again when she fell in love with him. And her dreams were no longer just that: all of them were very real.

'You have a delicious body, one of the most perfect I've ever seen—and I'm in the mood for you *right now*!'

The sharp slap on the flesh of Cat's bottom caused her lids to fly open, and she turned instinctively towards her husband, returning the passion of his good morning kiss before languidly kissing the warmth of his naked shoulder. As she did so her gaze was caught by the clock on the bedside table, her expression panicked as she pulled away from Caleb. 'Lucy shouldn't have slept this long,' she told him frantically. 'Something must be wrong——'

'Nothing is wrong.' He pulled her back down to his side. 'I got up and gave her a bottle over two hours ago.' His lips caressed the creamy length of her throat.

'You should have woken me,' she chided, although the worried tension left her body as she relaxed against him.

'There was no need to now that you're no longer feeding her yourself.' His mouth closed possessively over one turgid nipple.

Cat knew that he had missed this intimacy during the four months she had been able to feed their daughter herself, that he had indulged himself shamelessly since Lucy had been weaned on to a bottle.

Their eighteen months of marriage had agreed with them both, their beautiful daughter born five months ago, contrarily with Cat's green eyes and Caleb's dark colouring. Already she was charming all those about her, and Cat knew that the closeness Caleb had with both his children was doubly precious to him after the way he had almost lost Luke, the two men closer than they had ever been.

'Where is Lucy now?' she managed to gasp before she fell completely under her husband's sensual spell.

'Luke and Vikki took her for a walk,' Caleb murmured in a preoccupied voice. 'To give us old-timers a rest, he said,' he recalled in amusement. 'But he soon took that back when Vikki pointed out that you and she are the same age.'

Vikki and Luke had met at their wedding, and since that time a casual relationship had developed between them, deliberately kept that way by Vikki, her friend had confided to Cat. Luke had matured a lot the last eighteen months but, after the end of her casual relationship with Sam, Vikki wanted to be sure of him before committing herself to anything permanent between them. Cat was sure it was too late for that, the two of them obviously in love despite the five years difference in their ages, had started to tease Vikki about being her daughter-in-law!

Cat smiled up at Caleb. 'So we're all alone in the house,' she said invitingly, their nakedness reflected above.

'Except for a housekeeper, a couple of maids, four cats, and a dog,' he nodded mockingly. 'I know,' he acknowledged indulgently. 'You want our daughter to grow up in a happy domestic atmosphere. I just think keeping all of Sunny's kittens was a bit extreme.'

'She wouldn't have been happy if we had given them away,' Cat protested.

'Don't you think that right now we should be concentrating on making Mr and Mrs Steele happy?' he said throatily.

'What a lovely idea.' She moved into his arms, knowing that her reality with Caleb was better than any dreams could be: also knowing that if Harry could see the happiness she had known the last eighteen months as Caleb's wife that he would be happy for her, that he had helped make her the vibrantly beautiful woman she was today, the woman that was Caleb's love as he was hers.

Take 4 Exciting Books Absolutely FREE

Love, romance, intrigue... all are captured for you by Mills & Boon's top-selling authors. By becoming a regular reader of Mills & Boon's Romances you can enjoy 6 superb new titles every month plus a whole range of special benefits: your very own personal membership card, a free monthly newsletter packed with recipes, competitions, exclusive book offers and a monthly guide to the stars, plus extra bargain offers and big cash savings.

**AND an Introductory FREE GIFT for YOU.
Turn over the page for details.**

As a special introduction we will send you four exciting Mills & Boon Romances Free and without obligation when you complete and return this coupon.

At the same time we will reserve a subscription to Mills & Boon Reader Service for you. Every month, you will receive 6 of the very latest novels by leading Romantic Fiction authors, delivered direct to your door. You don't pay extra for delivery — postage and packing is always completely Free. There is no obligation or commitment — you can cancel your subscription at any time.

You have nothing to lose and a whole world of romance to gain.

Just fill in and post the coupon today to MILLS & BOON READER SERVICE, FREEPOST, P.O. BOX 236, CROYDON, SURREY CR9 9EL.

Please Note:- READERS IN SOUTH AFRICA write to Mills & Boon, Postbag X3010, Randburg 2125, S. Africa.

FREE BOOKS CERTIFICATE

To: Mills & Boon Reader Service, FREEPOST, P.O. Box 236, Croydon, Surrey CR9 9EL.

Please send me, free and without obligation, four Mills & Boon Romances, and reserve a Reader Service Subscription for me. If I decide to subscribe I shall, from the beginning of the month following my free parcel of books, receive six new books each month for £6.60, post and packing free. If I decide not to subscribe, I shall write to you within 10 days. The free books are mine to keep in any case. I understand that I may cancel my subscription at any time simply by writing to you. I am over 18 years of age.

Please write in BLOCK CAPITALS.

Signature _____

Name _____

Address _____

_____ Post code _____

SEND NO MONEY — TAKE NO RISKS.

Please don't forget to include your Postcode.

Remember, postcodes speed delivery. Offer applies in UK only and is not valid to present subscribers. Mills & Boon reserve the right to exercise discretion in granting membership. If price changes are necessary you will be notified.

6R   *Offer expires 31st March 1986.*

EP